# RESIN

Also by Amy Virginia Evans

Fantastically Fabulous February
Solstice Celebrations

# RESIN

Amy Virginia Evans

OPENAMUSE

ISBN 978-1490330839

Author Photo Credit: Ellen Sargent Korsh

For

Christus, Alexandra, Zoe, and Benjamin

—Nature's most exquisite gifts—

*Frigid.* Juliet's husband Skillman used this word to describe her behavior. He delivered it without malice. With characteristic tenderness and concern, he attributed her problem to what he believed was a medical ailment—ignorant of the term's archaic and misogynistic origin. Outwardly bristling, Juliet withered inside, acknowledging some truth to his accusation. After decades of steadfast marriage and vigilant child rearing, this emotional dead end seemed inevitable. At fifty-six years old, life's balance was no longer in Juliet's favor, and she could not envision escaping a bleak trajectory.

Pulling hard on the brass doorknob, she closed the door, stepping onto the granite landing and into the fresh snow covering her driveway. She walked past her quartz-blue Mercedes, its color hidden beneath white powder, then along the gravel alley between the backyards of Chestnut and Birchwood Streets. Glowing windows of familiar stately homes framed the movements of those who lived inside. Juliet no longer knew the names of the early risers. New neighbors had replaced those she had once known so well.

The wind picked up. Juliet welcomed its bite. Pulling her scarf closer and increasing her pace, she trampled over two empty lots, plunging onto the neglected trail leading into the Winston Town Forest.

There was a conventional road into town, with shoveled sidewalks, pedestrian crosswalks, and noisy school buses rumbling by twice daily, but Juliet shunned this route. Hopeful that nature would bolster her sagging spirit and offer relief from persistent fogginess, she had recently begun to explore these woods as a healthier way to reach downtown Winston.

Three decades ago, when Juliet and Skillman Grant searched for their first home, the proximity to the vast woods was a major factor in their final decision to move to this Massachusetts community. Every year, buyers paid exorbitant sums to secure a setting like this, so similar to the Berkshires, yet convenient to Boston. A Winston address was something to be envied.

Their three children had played in the Town Forest. Juliet would stand at the fringes and summon them home with a loud call between cupped hands. They would emerge with their friends, breathless, rosy-cheeked, and wild-eyed, invigorated by the magic of the woods. That was long ago. The forest was silent now.

With conviction, Juliet walked briskly along the snow covered path. She hardly noticed when its outline blurred until all evidence of it vanished. Straining to hear any sound of civilization, she calmed a rising panic. The clearing was unfamiliar. She circled it, scrutinizing the ground beneath the canopy of birches, pines, and maples, and the area around the damp trunk of a massive oak.

"Welcome."

Juliet spun around. A large man stood only a short distance away. He was tall, perhaps 6'6", and his weathered goose-down coat exaggerated his massive frame. Brilliant white hair and a full beard equally white set off his lightly tanned skin. Reflexively, she assessed her situation. She was far from help. A quick escape was improbable.

"I'm sorry," he said. "I didn't mean to scare you."

"I think I wandered off the path," she stammered.

"Charles Westfall." He nodded toward her in a gesture of acquaintance. "This land was my uncle's. I came here as a boy. Haven't been back since." His cadence was slow, his voice deep.

Juliet's eyes darted around. She wondered if she should run, but didn't know to where. Cordiality seemed her safest exit strategy.

She said, "Are you planning on building here now?"

"No, I like living this way."

With a sweep of his long arm, he directed her attention to an area behind him where a mottled brown tent was staked on level ground at the center of a rough campsite. Beyond that, at the edge of the partially frozen reservoir, sat a tiny dilapidated cottage. Several tiles of the slate roof were missing and many of the remaining ones had shifted out of place. The siding appeared to have been previously painted but was now gray as the slate. Uneven shutter remnants hung at awkward angles around tiny windows whose old glass was unbroken and reflected light off the icy pond. The front door was missing. At its threshold, a raccoon appeared, holding something in its hands. Juliet watched it pop the treasure into its mouth, then waddle off into the woods.

Shifting her boots in the snow, she returned her attention to the man. He was leaning against a peeling birch tree, one ankle crossed over the other, his expression open, his smile bemused. His focus was intense and entirely on her.

"I should go," she said, abruptly turning toward the direction she hoped was Concord Street.

"Tack about ten degrees northwest," he said.

Juliet looked back at him.

"Head a bit to your left. Hug the bank of the stream and you'll get there."

"Thanks. Sorry to bother you."

"Don't worry about it," he called after her. "You can walk this way anytime."

Setting out in the correct direction, Juliet walked less than twenty minutes before finally stepping out of the woods and into the rising bustle of Concord Street and downtown Winston. Soon she would see the big "T" at the platform and wait for a train that rarely arrived on schedule. Her destination, the Dyson Health and Fitness Center, was only one stop away but the eight mile distance was too far to walk. On Tuesdays and Thursdays, she attended Pilates class at the Center. On Mondays and Wednesdays, there was yoga. Today was Friday, which meant swimming.

Crossing the street, she joined the dreary collage of commuters, their brown, black, and navy winter coats huddled together against the cold, like horses on a windswept field. Once the train arrived, she pushed her way through the doors and claimed a crackled leather window seat.

Juliet loosened the cashmere scarf around her neck and focused on the sand-plastered boots covering the feet of a man seated across from her, then surrendered herself to the cabin's gentle rocking motion.

Hers was a classic beauty: statuesque, with shoulder length graying blonde hair, cool blue eyes and a willowy frame. Several passengers glanced at her admiringly, but Juliet took no notice.

When the conductor announced her stop, she joined the throngs of people on the street, each one appearing to have a purpose that somehow eluded Juliet.

Inside the Dyson Center, she changed into her swimsuit and then pulled open the heavy door to the pool. The blue water was still. Across the room, floor to ceiling windows were foggy with steam at deck level, but when Juliet looked up, she saw the soaring points of snow-covered pine trees outside. The moist, muffled air at the pool soothed her like a womb, just as it always did. Hadn't she offered similar comfort to her children during the years when boundaries between mother and child blurred under relentless needs? She took a deep breath, then exhaled forcefully, reminding herself for a countless time that the children had grown and moved away. Juliet could do whatever she wanted, whenever she chose.

She dove into the lukewarm water, kicked a few laps behind a flutter board, then tossed it onto the tile deck, settling into a rhythmic crawl.

One two, breathe. One, two, breathe.

Many problems had been solved while swimming, but one persisted, pulling heavily at her now. It was not the children, the house, the retirement package, or her career. It was her personal history she found most troubling. No part of it was exclusively hers anymore. Her own story had come to an end before she had truly lived it. Regardless of the cause, she knew sustaining this tired inner dialogue was sheer indulgence. She and Skillman had thirty years together. Anyone would consider them good years. Hadn't their children turned out well? Didn't their house appreciate in value? Wasn't their stable marriage a good example to family and community?

At the end of the pool, Juliet grabbed the polished concrete ledge and turned to check the clock on the wall. Fifteen minutes left to complete one mile. With a mighty thrust, she pushed off against the smooth tiles.

She was ashamed to admit how fiercely she struggled with self-actualization. Surely the window for individual exploration was closed after five decades. If her pulse would never again rise in sumptuous anticipation of some personal event or great unknown, then it was the logical consequence of her chronic emotional paralysis and insufficient courage to alter her own life's course. She recognized that harsh reality. She had only herself to blame.

Juliet pulled herself up the ladder and headed toward the locker room, then got dressed and left the Center.

At midday, quaint Concord Street bustled with community life. There were little coffee shops and tiny bookstores situated along brick sidewalks and narrow side streets. Colorful seasonal banners hung from lampposts along the way. In springtime, large planters outside each shop would overflow with gorgeous displays of cheerful pansies and assorted greenery. Just last year, the New York Times listed Winston as one of the country's most desirable communities, scoring high on all important indicators such as good schools, short commute, and low crime.

Juliet stopped at the popular Blersch's Market. She emerged a short while later carrying her reusable bags filled with organic eggs, extra virgin olive oil, red leaf lettuce, and a bottle of quality Merlot. She crossed the street to begin the long walk home.

"Juliet!"

Recognizing the clipped tone, Juliet tensed, then stopped and turned, facing the immaculately groomed, always prepared, Tanzy Lynch.

"We missed you at last night's meeting. Are you feeling better?" Tanzy asked, eyes fluttering momentarily from Juliet's face, assessing her appearance, head-to-toe.

"I am, thanks."

"You've been such a strong supporter of the Center. I hate to see any decisions made without you. I'll send you the minutes as soon as I get to the office. We're all so looking forward to hearing your cello at the benefit."

"Thanks, Tanzy. Sorry I can't chat more. I've got an appointment."

"Very good. We'll see you at the next meeting then, if not before."

Last night's Royce Art Center board meeting wasn't the first commitment she had recently skipped. It was tempting to avoid obligations while Skillman was away. She didn't have to explain her lack of enthusiasm to him or anyone else.

Her husband would not criticize her for this. Instead, he would wrinkle his forehead and ask if everything was okay, and was it anything he had said or done to upset her?

Juliet shifted the bags in her hands and set out again down Concord Street. The previously gloomy day had turned magnificent. Sunlight burst through scattered clouds, infusing the mid-winter sky with a pink glow and unseasonable warmth. At the downtown entrance to the Town Forest, Juliet set her bags onto the sidewalk in order to loosen her coat. With one foot already on the path, she remembered the morning's encounter deep in the woods. She decided this would not thwart her resolve to take the woods route home instead of walking on the street, but wondered exactly how much contact someone who appeared to be a hermit would tolerate. The man had not been threatening—even encouraging her to continue walking this way. Regardless of that assurance, she vowed to remain cautious.

After several minutes of following her earlier footprints, Juliet arrived at the same birch grove where she had stopped that morning. The grove was now empty. She forged on, over the melting snow, focusing primarily on the slippery path, still alert for signs of the man. At a cracking noise to her right, she turned.

He was some distance away, with his back toward her, unaware of her presence. She watched him position one piece of wood onto a large chopping block, already surrounded by several neat rows of split logs. Although the air temperature was still relatively low, he had removed his shirt and hung it over the branch of a nearby tree. The skin on his broad back was slick with sweat. He grabbed the ax, then heaved it up and back and down. Each time a log split, he replaced it, then split a new one. He worked in a steady rhythm. His muscled back bulged and rippled with the violence of the act.

Like a bow huntress with a deer in sight, Juliet held herself perfectly still. She could hear his panting breath while her own grew shallow and rapid.

Juliet turned without a sound and continued to retrace her footsteps through the woods to her home.

Standing at the kitchen counter, Juliet took a sip of fragrant hot tea then listened to her phone messages. One was from the Royce Art Center, with new details about the upcoming gala. The other was from Althea.

At twenty eight, Juliet's oldest child's life was infinitely more busy and complex than she remembered her own at that age. Althea was already a successful chiropractor at a holistic health center in Berkeley, California.

Juliet picked up the phone and punched in her number. When the receptionist answered, she asked to speak with Doctor Grant. In a moment, the sweet sound of her daughter's voice tugged at her heart.

"Thanks for calling me back so quickly. I can't talk long because I've got a patient waiting, but guess what? Dr. Lee will cover for me so I can make it to the gala."

"That's wonderful!"

"Are you nervous about performing at the Royce?"

"A little, because I've never played for a big audience before but if I keep practicing, I know everything will be okay."

"That's the attitude! What else is going on?"

Althea's tone was upbeat. Despite the geographic distance between them, she had read her mother's mood and sensed her need for cheer.

"Not much. I went swimming today, started working on a new necklace... Honestly, I'm not being that productive."

During her most recent trip to visit her daughter, Juliet sampled a few alternative treatments at Althea's office. The massage and reflexology sessions were pleasant, but at the conclusion of the Reiki session, she was overcome by tears. The kind practitioner assured her it was simply a healthy release of repressed emotion.

"Mom, I'm so sorry but now I have to see that patient. I'll let you know as soon as I book my flight to Boston. Have a good day! Love you."

"I love you, too, Sweetie."

Juliet gently put down the phone.

Althea was a joy. Even as a little girl, she always looked for opportunity and adventure. By the time she started first grade, it seemed almost as if she didn't need any more mothering. Her son Jonus was three then, and Juliet was pregnant with Deirdre.

So many details about family life had grown fuzzy. Her primary desire had always been to provide her children with happiness and a sense of purpose but that goal came with a price. Although she hoped she had done the best she could, Juliet knew in her heart she should have done better.

She thought back to when she first met Skillman Grant. She was twenty-five and working temporarily in the brick building located next to his Boston law firm. She was preparing a new satellite office for the transfer of 150 engineers and support staff. The change of pace was exhilarating; she was full of vigor and promise, glowing with anticipation about life's possibilities.

On that long ago afternoon, Juliet's boss asked her to deliver several packages to the mail service located on the other side of Skillman's law office. She wore an ivory-colored raw silk suit that accentuated her blond hair and fair complexion. As she hurried by the firm's entrance, Skillman Grant stepped headlong out of the revolving doors. The resulting collision between the two of them was as predictable as a movie scene.

"I'm so sorry!" Juliet said, stooping to pick up her packages.

"Don't worry about it," Skillman replied, a little gruffly, kneeling next to her. His expression changed to delight as a sun drenched Juliet came into focus. "Can I help you carry these somewhere?"

Her first impulse was to refuse, but she surprised herself. "Thank you. That would be really nice. I guess I should have made two trips."

Skillman never missed the chance to say that this day was the best of his life. Ever since then, his love seemed boundless. She loved Skillman, too, Juliet reminded herself.

With a sigh, she looked down at an empty mug, wondering where the tea had gone, then set it on the bottom of the porcelain sink. She'd wash it later.

Opening the basement door, she descended the stairs to her jewelry workshop, then spread new project materials and tools over the bench. In the center was a large oval-shaped piece of amber, about two inches long and an inch wide. It had arrived from Poland only a few weeks earlier. Juliet held the perfect specimen of cognac succinite up to the light. The translucent color reminded her of a corn field, deep in the afternoon, the sun lingering just above the horizon. She had seen a field like that in Nebraska during a cross-country road trip long ago. The late September air had warmed her skin as she stepped out of the car onto the dusty red dirt. A hint of decay from the field of spent stalks floated in the air.

The piece of Baltic amber now in her hand was probably 50 million years old, the fossilized resin of prehistoric trees. Cool and smooth, she rolled it over and over in her palm. She would design a necklace around the stone and make a bold statement; an unforgettable display. This was one piece of jewelry she did not intend to sell, and serendipitously, the perfect dress to set it off was already in her closet.

Successful at garnering an enthusiastic following for her work, Juliet had carved a comfortable niche for herself in the handmade jewelry community. If necessary, she could live modestly off the income earned from her craft. She fingered a business card resting on the shelf next to her, silently mouthing the name of the New York City distributor. So impressed was he with her talent, this influential man had offered her a work space and gallery in the SoHo district. Upon receiving this proposal, she had immediately dismissed the prospect of moving to New York; nonetheless, she valued the evidence of her marketability.

Intermittent sounds from the creaky bench made good company as she worked with the pliers and other tools, twisting silver strands into an intricate braid to form a loop around the amber focal piece. Hours later, when heavy footsteps overhead announced Skillman's arrival home, Juliet pursed her lips and began to clean up the tools and various pieces of the necklace.

Although her husband was always respectful of her time, he had broken the spell.

"Juliet?" Skillman called down to her from the top of the stairs.

"Hi, Skill! I'm at my workbench. Be right up!"

She caressed the amber oval one last time, slipped it into the small velvet bag, and headed upstairs to the kitchen.

"How was your trip?" She touched his arm lightly and kissed his cheek. Juliet tried to sound bright and interested. It made things so much easier.

"Actually, everything was quite productive. The merger is finalized so we won't have to meet again until the end of the year. I really hate that flight, though." Skillman tenderly brushed a strand of hair off Juliet's face. "You look so relaxed, my Jewell. How's the workshop going?"

He was always interested in the details of her life but Juliet tensed at what she perceived as his need to draw from her creative vein. Even so, she conjured up as much enthusiasm as she could. "Everything is great. Sorry I missed your call. Althea called, too. She'll be here for the benefit. Do you think we should have her take the airport limo?"

"Definitely." Skillman liked to make decisions about small things. "What have you heard from the other kids?"

"Jonus will be here but I haven't heard back from Deirdre.

"You know she always waits until the last minute."

"You're right." She glanced at the clock on the wall. "I'm starved. I don't think I've eaten since breakfast. Why don't you unpack and I'll get supper going?"

Juliet turned toward the counter, her hand already on the knob of a partially opened cabinet.

"What's the rush? I'd rather nibble on you right now." Skillman pressed his torso against her back and wrapped his arms around her waist. "I missed you, Jewels."

She twisted, kissed him on the cheek, then turned back to supper preparation. "I missed you too, Skill."

A second or two passed. He kissed the back of her neck, then silently left the room.

This was how it had been between them for years. Not terribly bad, but not good, either. She knew how painfully disappointed Skillman was. He loved her and wanted to be close to her. Even though it clearly was a mutual heartache, they rarely spoke about it. Juliet avoided the topic whenever possible. What was the point? It would only hurt and upset them both.

She dared to imagine life without Skillman on several occasions, usually after a glass of wine left her feeling expansive. With the mellowing of alcohol, the prospect was alternately exhilarating and frightening. And now, quite recently, something new and unsettling had been added to their mix. It was a creeping awareness that Skillman was applying his brakes, setting things aside for an eventual slowdown: retirement. How could he be ready to stop when she felt she had not yet begun?

Into the mixing bowl, she combined the frothy yeast with flour, attached the dough hook, then started the motor. When the kids were young, she always made bread from scratch; kneading it by hand, pummeling and pulling the heavy dough until all of the stress left her body, and the dough achieved the perfect texture of an earlobe. Now, the powerful mixer effortlessly accomplished this task. Tonight, she and Skillman would dine on this freshly baked focaccia, as well as broccoli-stuffed sweet potatoes drizzled with cheese.

When she heard her husband's footsteps on the stairway again, she uncorked the bottle of Merlot and filled her glass to the rim. It would be another quiet evening at home. Just the two of them.

With each opened door, Juliet encountered identical filth. Rushing from one stall to another, she found every toilet in the crowded public bathroom overflowing. Where could she relieve herself?

"Juliet...Juliet!"

"What?" Juliet blinked a few times until Skillman's face came into focus. Bright light breaking through a crack between the heavy ivory damask curtains cast a white sliver over the bed.

"I think you were having a nightmare." Skillman scanned her face, concerned.

"I don't know why I keep having that dream."

"Which one?"

She shook her head in disgust. "The infamous bathroom dream."

She had already researched its meaning. It represented a need to cleanse, both emotionally and physically, as well as an instinctual urge to remake oneself into something new. Alternatively, it meant she actually required a visit to the bathroom. Readjusting herself in anticipation of a few more delicious minutes of sleep, Juliet pulled the blanket and comforter up to her neck.

Skillman began to stroke her stomach.

"Juliet."

"Mmm?"

"Let's make love."

That was all it took for Juliet to become fully awake.

"Oh, Skill, I have so much to do today! I really should get into the shower right now. How about tonight?"

Juliet threw off the covers and stood next to the bed, smoothing the sheets on her side.

Skillman rolled onto his back. "We need to talk about us."

"I know. Let me do what I need to do this morning, then we'll talk this afternoon."

Juliet hugged a fresh bath towel in her arms.

Skillman's cheeks undulated with the unconscious habit of grinding his teeth. She bent over and kissed him on his temple, then moved toward the bathroom, shutting the door behind her to discourage further attention.

Truthfully, she had lost all interest in sex. Recent intimate encounters with Skillman left her annoyed and frustrated. With waning libido and plummeting estrogen levels, Juliet thought she would happily abandon sex completely.

At what point would her husband decide he had enough? Or more accurately, not had enough. With his frequent traveling, he could easily find comfort elsewhere, and a willing partner would not be difficult to attract. There were many women her age who would love to romance this neatly groomed and well-mannered fifty-seven year old man. Of course, even those ladies would be wasting their efforts. Men never had to settle for someone their own age. Juliet felt certain her husband wouldn't respond to any advances though; his strongest and weakest characteristic was unfailing faithfulness to family and friends.

Skillman had delivered a mug of hot tea to the top of her bureau while she was in the shower. Earl Grey, with milk and sugar; just the way she liked it. Juliet took a sip.

How could she not love this man? His needs were simple: companionship, attention, affection, and a desire to see a reflection of his best self in his woman's eyes. Why was this so difficult for her to deliver?

The back side of their house was pleasant on a cold Sunday morning. In a corner of the room, a cafe table anchored an intimate nook at the intersection of two windows. Bottom-up blinds covered the lower glass, providing privacy from the alley. Daylight streamed in at the top and filled the kitchen with energy. Juliet sat down and spread a cloth napkin over her lap while Skillman set a steaming plate in front of her. At the center was a toasted bagel covered with a neat mound of bright yellow scrambled eggs. A fresh sprig of parsley sprouted from the top. Artfully arranged around the plate's rim were tiny veggie-sausage circles.

"You're a master of comfort food." Juliet smiled up at him.

"Whatever it takes to please the Queen." He smiled back. "Do you still want to go to church?"

"Yes, let's do. We haven't been for weeks. They probably wonder what happened to us."

It was a short walk to the building that housed the stately Unitarian Universalist Fellowship of Winston, a historic example of classic New England church architecture, complete with original wavy glass and massive oak doors. Juliet and Skillman became UU members twenty years earlier in an effort to offer their kids a spiritual community and some religious education through this established Protestant offshoot. With thinking people like Thomas Jefferson and Florence Nightingale among the list of respected Unitarians, they considered themselves in good company.

Inside the foyer, they stamped snow off their feet, then walked down the center of the sanctuary to their favorite pew located on the left, four rows from the front. It was a sparse interior, reflecting the denomination's intellectual heritage. The walls, painted a muted white, contrasted nicely with original oak floors that gleamed from decades of diligent upkeep. Red velvet cushions softened hard benches. The blazing sun draped silhouettes of bare trees over their surfaces. When the organ prelude shook the room, the sanctuary quickly filled. Skillman took Juliet's hand and squeezed it tight.

I t was a cold Monday morning. Shoulder set hard into the wind, Juliet hurried down the empty alleyway. Snow that swept from the smooth white plain of connecting backyards formed miniature cyclones and blasted stinging particles everywhere. At the vacant lots, she turned left, enduring one last gust of bitter wind until the trees provided shelter. In seconds, the only sound was the creaking of tall pines as their tips swayed back and forth against a cerulean sky. After a few minutes of brisk walking, she arrived at the place where the path and campsite intersected. Charles Westfall was there, sitting on a flat black rock, stoking a small fire. He looked up and smiled.

She had planned to exchange a polite greeting and quickly pass by him as she made her way through the woods to the train and the Dyson Center.

"Good morning!" he boomed, rising to greet her. "Would you like a cup of tea?"

"I...ah...sure. I guess I could. It would feel good to warm up a bit." There was really no reason to refuse his hospitality.

Charles turned back toward the fire, lifted the steaming black kettle off the hook and poured water into a battered tin mug.

"Thank you," she said, taking the mug from him.

A whiff of something familiar was in the air. She looked down at the cup where leaves floated on the surface of the water.

"Keep it level and wait a few minutes for it to steep," he told her. "The leaves will sink to the bottom. They'll stay there for good unless you stir them up."

"All right." Juliet held the cup close to her face and let the steam warm her chin. "This smells like Earl Grey tea. Is there bergamot in it?"

"It's bee-balm. Wild bergamot."

"Hmm. Interesting." Juliet smiled politely. "Don't you get cold out here?"

"Sometimes. I just head into the lodge if it's really bitter." He gestured toward his tent.

Juliet laughed. "You don't consider this really bitter?"

"Not especially. Acclimation helps. The weather will take you down if you give it a chance, though."

Juliet cautiously tipped the hot mug toward her lips, took a tentative sip, then smiled. "This is really good."

"Surprised?"

"Well, I've never actually had flower tea in the woods."

They were silent for a while, both nursing their drinks. Each warm exhale delivered puffy little clouds that rose to meet one another but never quite connected. In the glade, the wind was minimal, but the cold air still penetrated. Charles stood a few feet away; one hand in his pocket, the other holding his mug. He had achieved some happy medium between clean and completely unkempt. Juliet was surprised to find him attractive, in a rough sort of way; not at all what she'd expected from a homeless man.

"Do you stay here in the woods all day?" she ventured.

"Pretty much. I have everything I need. I like to live off the land. Use what I find around me."

She glanced about the campsite.

"I'm on my way to a health club right now. That must sound pretty ridiculous to you."

"Not at all. What will you do there?"

"Well, today it's hot yoga and meditation; tomorrow, Pilates; and on Fridays, I swim."

"Impressive. What's your favorite stroke?" Charles asked.

"Everything except the butterfly. Mostly, I just like being in the water. It feels so free."

Juliet felt the blood rush to her cheeks, embarrassed to have revealed something personal.

Her mug was nearly empty. "Well, I'd better get going. Thanks so much for the tea. It's Charles, right?"

"Yes, Charles. Charles Westfall," he said.

He had not moved from the spot where he poured and served her tea.

"Well. Bye, then," Juliet said, handing him the mug.

"Good bye."

As she walked down the path toward Concord Street, she felt herself being watched, and did not find the sensation entirely unpleasant.

At her workbench later that afternoon, Juliet untied the crimson ribbon that cinched the velvet bag, then placed its contents onto the flocked concept board. Her original design featured the polished amber piece suspended from three circles of memory wire, strung with alternating tiny cube and bicone beads. Last night, a more stunning idea came to her: a matinée length lariat ending with the oval succinite surrounded by a multitude of semi-precious gemstones.

Inside a box of hundreds of neatly organized beads, she found the perfect colors and shapes to enhance the large cognac-colored focal piece. She positioned several matching amethyst-colored drop beads into the grooves of the board, then added a few lapis lazuli rice beads at regular intervals. Garnet-colored glass cubes, ivory colored lamp-work beads, and sterling silver balls pulled it all together. Juliet would purchase semi-precious stones at the bead store tomorrow to replace these glass dummies. It was an extravagant splurge. She couldn't recall the last time she allowed herself to keep one of her own creations. Listing all of the materials needed to complete the necklace, she put her tools away and walked back upstairs.

Considering the morning's brilliant sunshine, Juliet was surprised to see how much the weather had deteriorated. It had apparently been snowing hard all afternoon. Gas street lights on Chestnut Street were already glowing and now the road resembled a nineteenth century picture postcard. Standing at the front window next to the radiator, cozy and protected from the elements, her thoughts wandered to the earlier encounter with Charles Westfall. Tea with the hermit had been an unexpectedly pleasant experience. His grounded manner and steady speech were calming, almost reassuring, although the intensity of his focus was strangely at odds with the peaceful aura surrounding him. She imagined a mysterious story attached to his life, rich with difficult twists and turns. This reverie ended abruptly when she realized, unlike herself, Charles was actually outside in the midst of the blizzard.

At the thought, she bounded up two flights of stairs to the chilly attic where a small window provided a view of her neighbors' roofs and the trees of the Town Forest. Shivering, Juliet hugged herself tight while pressing her left cheek against the smooth glass. She looked to the right as far as the wooden frame allowed and strained to recognize any sign of Charles' campsite. Although she searched for a streak of smoke wafting over the black tree tops, it was impossible to recognize anything definitive through the swirling snow.

Standing amid the myriad of boxes and crates, she surveyed the area for something Charles might find useful at his campsite. Her eyes landed on a striped wool blanket draped over an old dresser. Spreading it out on the floor for inspection, she discovered a few jagged moth holes, but declared it otherwise sound. Although there was a possibility he'd be insulted by her charitable gesture, Juliet decided she'd take that risk and offer it to him tomorrow on her way to the bead shop. After locating a cast-off sweatshirt to warm herself, Juliet continued to poke around, investigating the contents of dust covered boxes; foraging in her attic for anything potentially useful to a man living in the woods.

Skillman smiled, looking out the window and wondering how any morning could be more delightful. Overnight, a half foot of snow punctuated the landscape with improbable drifts and unique shapes where it formed mounds over bushes and large rocks. Music reverberated throughout the house as Juliet worked her cello through one of the Bach Cello Suites in the living room below. Skillman took the back stairs to the kitchen, filled the kettle with water, and waited for a stanza break.

"Good morning, Jewels!"

"Morning."

"Want any tea?"

"No thanks, Skill. I'll probably have some later."

He walked through the doorway, peeling a banana, then leaned over and kissed her.

"What's on tap for my girl today?"

She adjusted her sheet music.

"Well, I'm going to finish practicing this and after my shower I'll go to Pilates, then Bead It to pick up a few beads for that amber necklace I'm working on. I'm having lunch with Susan, too. How about you?"

"Just a regular day," he answered. "You're going to take a shower before you go to the Dyson Center?"

"You know me, Skill. I can never be too clean. I like fresh sweat on clean skin."

"Mmm. I'd like a taste of that skin." Skill winked at her.

Juliet craned her neck to view the kitchen clock through the doorway. "Aren't you going to be late?"

"Yes, I'd better get going. Well, have a great day, Jewels. Love you." He kissed her on the mouth.

"I love you, too."

She heard the door shut and watched his car pull out of the driveway, then down the alley. Juliet felt her shoulders relax. The phone was ringing but she was in no mood to answer. She absently listened for the caller's message.

"I know you're there. Pick up. I see you!" the voice on the other end taunted.

With lightning speed, Juliet put her cello down and ran to grab the phone.

"Glennie!"

"Juliet!"

"Where are you now?"

"I'm at Heathrow getting my luggage but I couldn't wait another minute to call."

"Oh Glennie, you're so sweet. How was the ashram?"

"Fabulous. Way better than I expected. I learned so much, Juliet. Everything was glorious."

"Oh, I can't wait to hear all about it! When will—"

"Sorry, Juliet," Glennie interrupted. "I just saw one of my bags fall off the turnstile and I know Peter is probably pacing back and forth waiting for me."

"Promise to call me the minute you're back in Winston, okay?"

"Absolutely! Talk soon! Bye!"

Juliet hung up the phone and smiled. Her dearest friend Glennie had been in India for two months, incommunicado. It would be wonderful to have her back in Winston soon. She knew she was fortunate to have found someone with whom she meshed so perfectly.

Glennie collected her bags, cleared customs and walked quickly out to the airport lobby where Peter waited. When they hugged, it was Glennie who squeezed hardest.

"You must be exhausted," Peter offered as they walked outside.

"I am but it's so good to be here with you." She gave his arm a squeeze.

"Well, did you learn anything from the yogis?"

Glennie turned sharply. From the condescending tone and the look on his face, it was clear he was being sarcastic. So, this is the way it's going to be, she thought. Even after all this time apart, nothing was different. She knew it would be a long haul to salvage her marriage, but it was her new priority. The past few years had been full of nitpicking and bickering; stark contrast to how Glennie hoped to live her life. In spite of that, she wasn't ready to abandon this relationship. She didn't want to grow into a grandmother without a grandfather beside her to share the joy. She and Peter had been happy years ago; she had faith they could find that love again. Meeting him here in London to spend a few days together before going home would hopefully help them reconnect. Glennie was determined.

"I learned so much. I can't wait to share it with my students," she finally responded.

# RESIN

. . . . . . . .

Dressed for the day, Juliet was halfway out the door when she remembered the cast-off blanket she planned to give Charles, so she ran up the attic stairs to retrieve it, then finally left home to resume her schedule.

The alley's winding configuration concealed the entrance to the path from most of the neighborhood. Only Claire Houghton, who lived at Seventeen Chestnut Street, directly opposite the vacant lots, could see Juliet enter the path, and then only if she happened to look out her kitchen window at exactly the right moment. The kind old woman would not be one to gossip. It seemed Charles Westfall's living arrangement was undetected by Winston and Juliet thought it best to keep it that way.

For the second time in only a few days, fresh snow obscured the path through the woods leading to the campsite. Fortunately, during her previous walks, she had the foresight to identify natural guideposts situated above the snow line. Periodically, she stopped to check these bearings. Above her, a blue sky crisply defined everything beneath it. Here and there, a birch tree bowed over, bent from the weight of accumulated snow. The beauty of this post snowstorm day in New England was spectacular, and although Juliet did not readily admit many positives about winter, even she was awed by such splendor.

The minute she arrived at the clearing, Charles Westfall greeted her from his seat by the campfire.

"Good morning," he said. "I was hoping I'd see you today. Your tea is ready."

"Really? That's so nice of you."

Although Juliet appreciated his warm reception, she was surprised by his brazen expectation that he would see her again.

Charles met her halfway, handing her the identical battered tin mug used the day before.

Juliet took a sip.

"This sure tastes good on a chilly day. Thanks so much."

"You're very welcome."

She offered a tentative smile, then surveyed the area around the campsite, amazed at how much fresh snow was piled outside the tent.

"Was it difficult out here in the storm last night with the wind blowing and everything?"

"No. I was fine. It's actually very snug in the tent. It's only temporary, though. The cottage is almost ready."

He pointed to the area behind her.

She turned to look at the tiny building.

"Wow. I can see the improvement. It must be very old," Juliet commented.

"It is. It's been here for quite a while. My grandfather and uncle built it."

Charles and Juliet took a few steps together in that direction.

"Do you want to see the inside?" He gestured toward the entryway, now covered by a battered tarp.

Juliet weighed his proposal. Before her could be someone who was exactly as he appeared: a very polite, very handsome, very capable outdoorsman. Or not. Despite her ease in his presence, she reminded herself to be careful.

"Sure," she answered, taking a gamble.

"Let's look at the outside first," he commanded, walking ahead of her toward the cottage. Juliet followed in his footsteps, her black leather boots swallowed by indentations he left in the snow.

"Back in my grandfather's time, people built their own homes. They were designed to last for generations." He pointed to the granite slabs that supplied the foundation. "I imagine they pulled these pieces in by draft horse. The rest of the material was probably cut from the woods around us."

"Do you think it was just the two of them or did they have help?" Juliet asked.

"Family legend says it was just them. They were hardy souls."

When they reached the makeshift doorway, Charles held open the flap and stood aside, inviting Juliet to move through the opening first.

She entered another realm. Light filtered through the rough window glass, washing everything in a golden glow. To her right, a coarse table made of sturdy oak logs was pushed up against the wall. Two flattened stumps positioned at either end of the table functioned as stools. On the far wall, several handmade shelves were neatly stocked with tools and supplies. There was a hand-hewn bed, its frame raised a few inches off the ground and its top covered with multiple patchwork furs. One corner of the room was partitioned by a cloth suspended from the ceiling. An enormous fireplace held the promise of warmth. Juliet moved closer to inspect it.

Charles stood by the door, observing Juliet.

"What do you think?" he asked.

She turned to him.

"It's nothing like I expected. It's going to be cozy and comfortable in here."

Charles nodded.

"And here are my supplies."

He crossed the sloping wood floor and arrived at the three shelves. Juliet followed him, stepping around a tidy pile of tools.

"The top shelves are for all my dried food." He pointed to the various containers. "There's a reason for this kind of storage. Animals are constantly foraging but if they can't smell anything, they won't bother investigating. That's why everything is wrapped so well. Down here," he said, pointing to the next shelf, "are some modern conveniences. I have cans of food and also a water purifier for when I need one."

"This is incredible. Do you use the water from the reservoir?" asked Juliet.

"No. It's easier to pull it up from the old well I found near the outer path."

Juliet cocked her head. "I didn't even notice it'd been reopened when I walked by last week. I had no idea you were here."

They looked at each other and smiled.

Juliet touched a container on the shelf.

"What's this?"

"Dried rose hips. They're very high in Vitamin C."

She further surveyed the cottage interior.

"What's behind that curtain?"

"That," he said with a smile," is my bathroom."

Juliet lowered her eyes, embarrassed.

"There's a chamber pot behind there and a bowl and a towel."

The mention of a towel reminded her of the old blanket she carried in her leather bag.

"I brought something for you. It's a blanket I don't use anymore. I thought it might come in handy out here."

She wrestled it out of her bag and handed it to Charles.

Charles unfolded the blanket without taking his eyes off her, then stepped behind her and wrapped it around her shoulders.

"This will help keep a visitor warm."

She could feel the heat of his hands where they rested briefly on her shoulders.

He walked around to face her again.

"Thank you for thinking of me."

"You're welcome."

The cottage was quiet. Never had she stood so close to such a physically powerful man. His radiating bulk made her feel small, feminine, and vulnerable, but surprisingly unafraid. Also impossible to ignore was a long dormant but distinct tingling sensation that grew stronger with each passing moment.

"I really should be going. I have to go to my Pilates class today," Juliet said.

"Of course," he replied. "I hope you'll visit again. I enjoy your company. I do have one question for you, though."

"Okay," said Juliet, with some trepidation.

"You've never told me your name."

Relieved, she laughed and smiled. "Oh, sorry about that. It's Juliet."

She took the blanket off her shoulders, handed it to him, then watched as he folded it neatly and draped it over the table situated next to the door. As he held the entry flap aside for her, streaming sunlight formed a bright triangle on the floor. Outside, Juliet struggled to readjust to the brightness, then turned to face Charles. The sun shone directly into his eyes. Thick black eyelashes framed beautiful green irises. A little patch of pink appeared on each of his cheeks. She remembered that she was supposed to speak.

"Thanks so much for the tour and the tea, Charles."

"My pleasure, Juliet."

She walked down the long path toward Concord Street for the third time. Charles was watching. She turned her head and gave him her sweetest smile.

After Pilates class, Juliet spent extra time at the Dyson Center washing her hair to remove the smoky smell. In the steamy warmth of the shower stall, absently lathering soap under her arms and around her breasts, she recalled the image of Charles in the morning light. The cadence of his voice. His eyes. The way he looked at her.

At Bead It, the clerk removed the tray from beneath the glass to display the variety of options on the counter top. When Juliet found precisely what she required, she paid the clerk, then tucked the precious package into her leather shoulder bag. Although she was looking forward to lunch with her friend, she was also impatient to return to her jewelry project later in the day.

It wasn't quite noon, but Susan was already seated at The Claret Cafe, enthusiastically waving through the spotless window. At the door, Juliet stopped to breathe in vanilla and coffee aromas mingled with the scent of logs burning in the expansive fireplace. Baskets of philodendrons suspended from the ceiling; bold columns of light shot around spiky green leaves of snake plants positioned on each window sill.

Juliet checked her coat in the foyer, then located Susan at a corner table. Chatter in the large room quieted as diners absently watched her walk across the room to observe who she would meet.

"Hi, Susan," Juliet said, pulling a chair over the wood floor.

"Juliet, you look absolutely stunning! I just love your sweater! How was your Pilates class?"

Grateful for small favors, she appreciated that Susan did not jump up with enthusiasm as she was known to do. Eyes were still upon them as Juliet settled onto her chair.

"Thanks. Everything is great. It's so good to see you. You must be really busy with your new job."

"It's a juggle, but manageable. Tea?" Susan gestured to the waitress. "So, how are the kids and Skillman?"

"They're all good. Skill is busy with his usual stuff. All three kids are hopefully coming home for the benefit. Can both you and Gil make it?"

"Are you kidding? We'd never miss your debut! Gil is absolutely impressed that you play the cello. He wishes I would pick up a hobby."

Susan's cheerful face clouded at the mention of her husband. The effort she exerted to make her life appear idyllic to others had loosened somewhat between the two women. Juliet considered this a breakthrough in their friendship.

When the tea arrived, Juliet added milk and sugar, glanced quickly at the ever evolving Claret Cafe menu, then rested it on the tablecloth.

"How are things between you two these days?" she asked.

"Better. I think the separation was a good idea. It forced us to stand back and take a look at who we had become. It was hard on Cliff and Carl, though. Even grown kids want their parents together."

When Susan's twins Cliff and Carl attended grade school with her son, Jonus, Susan whipped up a soccer carpool schedule that kept Juliet on track every week. Although the two women didn't seem to have much in common, Susan made the effort to maintain their relationship over the years and Juliet came to appreciate her sunny outlook. Her friend chattered incessantly, affording her the chance to completely relax. A steady diet of perky gab could be draining, but right now, it was the bright spot she needed.

The young waitress returned to take their orders. A tiny sapphire stud decorated her pierced nose. After she left, Juliet continued.

"And the job?"

"It's fabulous working at the Royce. It's perfect for me because I can still be an organizational control freak, but for a good cause." She smiled. "I love the leather couches in the gallery and the original art in the offices. I don't know how they do it and still have money left for staff and acquisitions."

Juliet sipped her tea. Because Susan had only recently been hired as the administrative assistant, she had not yet learned of her new employer's impending crisis. As a board member, Juliet was well aware of the Center's precarious financial situation. A steady source of funding from a local business had recently been withdrawn, creating a probability the Center might be forced to close its doors, at least temporarily. Juliet saw no need to worry Susan with such details, yet.

"It's a wonderful place, Susan, and I hope it stays that way forever."

"Me, too."

Susan gave Juliet a quick once-over look. "Now, tell me where you get your hair done these days. I just love the color!"

After lunch, the two friends parted. Juliet walked down the alley instead of through the woods. The idea of seeing Charles twice the same day seemed imprudent.

Later that afternoon, Skillman entered through their front door, unnoticed by Juliet. She was playing the cello, lost in concentration. He stood in the foyer, savoring the sound; imagining a much younger version of his wife, struggling to carry a big cello up the stairs to her music teacher's door. Because he had no music training, every performance sounded flawless to his ears. He marveled at her skill and the power she had to transport herself while playing. Juliet told him once that playing the cello was like meditating; she lost track of time and all awareness of her surroundings.

When she finished, the crisp tic-toc of the metronome persisted until she leaned over to silence it.

"I'm home," he called out in a soft voice.

"Hi, Sweetie," she replied, just as softly.

Juliet listened to the sound of his footsteps as he came around the corner.

"Hello Jewels."

"How was your day?" Juliet rested the cello in its stand, twisted the end of the bow to loosen the hair, then followed her husband into the kitchen.

"Good. Anything happen here?"

"Yeah, an email from Deirdre. There's a chance she'll be working and won't make it to the benefit."

"Oh, Jewels." Skillman raised his eyebrows, sympathetically. "You know the restaurant business. People come and go. Things change. Maybe she'll get away after all."

"You know, she's the only one of us who has real talent. Those Conservatory concerts of hers were inspiring. She's why I took up the cello again. I just wish she could be here."

Skillman reached over and put his arms around her.

How many times had they hugged this way in this very kitchen? During the early years of marriage, there were snatches of passion; fleeting moments of love caught between a baby crawling underfoot, or a toddler calling from another room. Later, the hugs were full of support as they reeled from the crash of a teenager slamming a door in anger, or stood next to an empty bed during a missed curfew. Now, it was just the two of them. Hugs had become almost too intimate for Juliet. She could feel the tension in her shoulders. She could feel her pelvis pull away. Ambivalence and confusion reigned whenever she was close to Skillman this way.

Juliet patted his back through his starched shirt one last time before detaching herself.

He smiled at her, forgiving it all. He was not a big man but Juliet knew that there were few men with bigger hearts. Skillman was just under six feet tall, just over 180 pounds, not much muscle, and a firmly established rounded belly. The few strands of gray in his light brown hair did not age him. Like many men, he somehow grew more attractive with every added year. Even the crow's feet around Skillman's eyes were endearing. He wasn't leaving anything to chance, though; Juliet knew his fastidious grooming was the extra effort he made to appeal specifically to her. She wished he could relax; be a little impulsive instead of meticulous and analytical. She encouraged him to stop shaving on weekends but it was rare that he would indulge her. He was concerned that people would think he was lazy.

Although Skillman would never criticize her appearance, she knew he was most proud of her when her hair was freshly highlighted and styled, and her nails manicured. Juliet agreed that scrupulous grooming was an important habit at her age. She stopped short of embracing this philosophy as enthusiastically as many of her peers, who spent hours every week at salons and spas, battling the inevitable.

She still looked exceptional, but she had long ago lost the ephemeral incandescence so effortless to a young woman. Gone was the glossy swing of heavy hair; the radiant vitality of healthy skin; the unmistakable allure of toned legs. Although the arrival of menopause had been a welcome relief from fluctuating hormones, Juliet waged constant war against the harridans in her head insisting she was old, and the best days of her life had passed.

There was a cosmopolitan feeling to Winston. Most of Juliet's needs were located within walking distance, so she traveled easily from errand to errand, a satchel slung over her shoulder, fantasizing about life in some culture-saturated European city. A sturdy but elegant leather bag was an important part of this persona. It dovetailed nicely with her modest commitment to environmentalism. Recycling, and avoiding the use of plastic bags were her primary contribution but she continued to place a high premium on comfort and the enjoyment of a full range of modern conveniences. Early in their relationship, she and Skillman had experimented with camping but just as quickly rejected the activity. Both found deliberate deprivation absurd in a modern era.

With an absence of urgency, she ambled along, absorbing Concord Street's pleasant sensations. There was the enticing smell of freshly baked chocolate-filled croissants from Le Petit Dejeuner; the tower of tightly bundled Persian rugs stacked outside Omar's Rug Shop; the brisk movements at Dress Your Best where the young clerk used her broom to dust snow off a hat-shaped mosaic embedded in the sidewalk.

Juliet stopped abruptly at the sparkling window of Cohort's Gallery. She knew this place well but there was a new painting on display. The 4x4 foot abstract oil set in an antique walnut burl frame was a sumptuous collision of colors: brick red, ocher, eggplant swirls tipped with glistening gold, azure and cream dappled with bold points of burgundy. Juliet felt the familiar swift response to work she loved—a visceral connection with its creator.

When she pulled open the ornate door of Cohort's Gallery, the playful notes of a flute sonata transported her to what she affectionately called Planet Art. Proprietor Rachel stood at the back of the store discussing a wire mobile with a customer. Juliet wandered across the gleaming wood floor, leisurely perusing the collection of art from all over the world, admiring Rachel's extraordinary gift for collecting genuinely unique expressions of beauty. Juliet allowed herself to soak it in.

In the corner was a sculpture juxtaposing black lava stones with polished pale driftwood. Next to it, a large elaborately glazed urn, set in almost invisible wire mesh, appeared to float over the brass pedestal beneath it. Numerous paintings of all sizes and media hung from the walls. Eventually, Juliet arrived at her favorite spot: the jewelry case. She zeroed in on a garnet ring and earring trio fashioned with sterling silver and delicate freshwater pearls. It was displayed on a cushion of olive-colored velvet.

"Spectacular, isn't it?"

Juliet turned to face Rachel, whose dark hair, pulled back off her face, exploded in shiny curls at the nape of her neck.

"I don't know how you find this beauty. You never cease to amaze me."

"Thank you, Juliet. That means a lot to me, especially from you. I can't believe talented Juliet Grant lives right here in Winston."

Juliet smiled. It was nice to be appreciated.

"Yesterday, I sold the amethyst necklace you made." Rachel's expression turned bittersweet.

"Oh, Rachel! You know all your treasures go to good homes."

"I find the art; I fall in love with it; I buy it. I spend hours gazing at it here every day. I decorate around it. It always seems so sudden and abrupt when it sells, though. Then, the love affair ends, and my heart is broken." She released a deep sigh.

Juliet arms gently circled Rachel's ample torso, then stepped back, holding her friend's hands in hers.

"I don't know when I'll have something new for you, Rachel. You know I always slump in the winter. I'm just about done with a piece right now, but for once, I'm not going to sell it."

The art curator made another sad face.

"Maybe I'll do something with turquoise in the spring. You can have that."

"Wonderful!" Rachel finally beamed. Please don't stay away until it's done, though. I love seeing you in here devouring the place with your pretty eyes."

"You know I'll be back soon," Juliet assured her. "By the way, what's the story behind that exquisite painting in the window? I'm swooning over the colors."

"I got it yesterday. The Royce called and asked me to pick it up. It was shipped to them already framed. There's no signature. No explanation." Both of them looked toward the window display. "I instantly felt it should be here. The mystery definitely seduced me. You know I like drama!" Rachel laughed, then touched the side of her eye with her fingertip. "I'll probably get my heart broken again when it sells!"

Juliet smiled indulgently at her friend. "How much are you asking for it?"

"Four thousand."

"Whoa." Juliet exhaled.

"I think it's worth it. It may be a hard sell because of the signature issue, but the quality is undeniable."

"Well, I love it. For my sake, I hope it doesn't sell too soon."

The gallery door opened and a young couple walked in.

"Juliet, I need to go. Please stay in touch!"

"I promise. Take care of yourself."

"You, too."

Rachel rushed over to greet the newcomers and Juliet eventually let herself out of the gallery.

It was early afternoon but Skillman was already home; another unusual break in his otherwise normal routine.

"What are you doing here so early?" Juliet asked, pulling off her boots and stowing them next to the kitchen door.

"Remember that merger in Tampa I worked on last month?"

"Yes?"

"Well, it collapsed. Now they want me to get down there ASAP to rescue the damn thing."

"That's too bad, Skill. But hey, it's Florida at least." Juliet smiled, encouragingly.

"You're right. It could definitely be worse."

He buckled the side of his bulging attaché case and pulled it off the counter. "I'll be home by Friday. Sorry I have to screech out of here but the flight is at five."

"It's okay. I hope everything goes well."

"Thanks. Love you," Skillman said, kissing her.

"Love you, too," Juliet said, closing the door after him.

Mid-morning sunlight filled Juliet's bedroom. With Skill away, it had been easy to devote her solitude to uninterrupted work on the necklace, so she did just that, late into the night. Because the early part of the day had already evaporated, there would be no visit to the Dyson Center for a workout. Instead, Juliet intended to stop by Cohort's Gallery and show Rachel her completed design, even though she knew her friend would plead with her to sell it. Although the thought of a hefty profit was tempting, Juliet would hold onto her resolve to keep this particular piece.

Once out of bed, she fluffed the pillows and arranged the brocade comforter evenly. As she considered her schedule, she thought she'd perhaps stop by and see Charles Westfall on her way home from Cohort's. She would pick up a few things at the grocery first. It really took no extra effort to pass through the woods afterward and she found conversation with someone outside the stifling social dynamic of Winston a refreshing diversion. It was difficult to imagine anyone in Winston responding to Charles the way she did. With closed minds, they would see an eccentric hermit. Juliet had moved beyond that perception. She now saw in Charles a delightful and intelligent gentleman. There could be no harm in that.

At the double-wide closet, she chose a garnet-colored cashmere sweater featuring single cables running down the sleeves and around the hem. She wanted to wear something that would not detract from the one-of-a-kind necklace she planned to show Rachel. Using the large dresser mirror as her guide, she fastened the lariat around her neck, smiling with satisfaction at her reflection. The jewels lay flat on her breastbone and contrasted well with the color of her smooth skin, but her sharp eye for balance suggested the precious amber suspended at the end could be further enhanced. In her top drawer, she rummaged for a long neglected black push-up bra, then put it on, smoothing her sweater and adjusting the necklace. Now, the stone fell between the two soft mounds rising and falling inside the opening of her neckline. Juliet stood there mesmerized, as if gazing at her reflection for the first time.

At Cohort's, Rachel gushed over Juliet's creation.

"Ah, it's gorgeous. Just as I knew it would be. With that necklace and your cleavage, nothing could be more beautiful. Ooh la la!"

Juliet giggled, refastening her coat. "I know I look ridiculous right now but I think this style and color would be perfect for evening."

"Can't you leave it with me for just a few days so everyone can appreciate it?" Rachel begged.

Juliet gently declined her request, promising again to start a new project right away. She'd bring in the competed work as soon as it was ready. On her way out, she paused at the gallery doorway, taking a few minutes to enjoy the beautiful painting she'd discovered just yesterday.

With her empty leather shoulder bag swinging at her side, she walked down the street toward Blersch's Natural Market, contemplating her solo dinner menu. When Skill was away, it hardly seemed necessary to trouble herself to cook, but she knew she should be mindful of her own nutritional needs.

The produce department burst with a cornucopia of options. She'd begin with several oranges to squeeze fresh for tomorrow's breakfast. As she handled the fruit, carefully selecting the best from the bunch, it occurred to her that Charles might like some oranges as well. After adding two more to the four already in her basket, she had second thoughts. Juliet returned the extra oranges to the bin and watched them roll back into position. Most certainly, Charles was unable to afford such a luxury. The last thing she wanted was to appear forward or overly charitable. On the other hand, who wouldn't appreciate fresh fruit? Juliet struck a compromise, adding one orange instead of two to her own supply, then completed the rest of her shopping and left the store.

At Concord Street, she nonchalantly scanned the area for any cars or pedestrians she recognized, then turned onto the path where it opened behind the gnarled oak tree. Within fifteen minutes, she was deep into the woods, nearly up to the far side of the clearing. She had passed the newly constructed lean-to where Charles stored his wood, noting the fresh evergreen boughs placed over the opening to block drifting snow.

When she arrived at the campsite, fire was smoldering inside the rock-rimmed pit by the tent, but Charles was nowhere to be seen. Juliet was uncertain how to announce herself. She didn't want to startle him by calling out his name, but the longer Juliet stood there, the more she felt she was invading his privacy. It was entirely possible he preferred to be left alone. Wasn't that a hermit's nature? One who sought company would live with someone else, not by himself. Her bag grew heavy on her shoulder. Losing her resolve, Juliet walked toward the path leading home.

"Juliet!"

Her heart skipped a beat at the sound of Charles' deep voice calling her name.

"Hi! I thought maybe you were taking a nap or something," Juliet said, turning back.

"I was down at the reservoir catching some fish."

Charles held up a string with a few fish dangling from it.

"Oh! Look at that! I didn't know you could catch fish in the winter."

Charles laid the yield on a large flat rock, then walked over to Juliet.

"I'm glad you stopped by. Can you stay for a while?"

"Yes. I can."

He knelt down to add a few logs to the fire. She stood behind him. From this vantage, she could see the top of his head. He had a thick mane of white hair but it had thinned just a bit at the crown. She jammed her hands in her pockets, fighting an impulse to reach down and touch him there.

Charles leaned closer to the fire, resting on his forearms, blowing hearty gusts of air toward the scarlet embers, until flames licked up and around the sides of the recently added logs. He stood again.

"Is there anything I can do to help?" asked Juliet.

"Sure. I'll show you how to hook up the tea kettle and then you'll know how to do it next time."

Charles walked over to the area where he stored the pots and pans.

Juliet was conflicted. It was presumptuous of him to assume she would continue these visits. Considering the contrast between their lives, Juliet found it an incredible display of ego. She didn't want to judge him, though. It could be that he was lonely and unconsciously employed overconfidence to compensate. As the fire at her feet increased in size and strength, the heat worked its way up her body until she felt herself relax. Maybe she could find a way to forgive his familiarity after all.

Charles showed her how to connect the swinging arm extension from where the tea kettle would dangle. He attached it to the post at the side of the pit, then helped her lift the heavy iron kettle, handing her a sturdy stick so she could more easily move it back and forth. She sat down next to him on a flat rock near the fire while they waited for the water to boil. The rock had absorbed some warmth and the heat again worked its way through her pants. The sudden shift again between cold and warm sent a shiver of pleasure down her spine.

"What have you been up to today, Juliet?" asked Charles.

"Not much, so far. I missed working out because I stayed up too late finishing a necklace. I did a few errands, though. How about you?"

"Not so fast. Are you an artist?" he asked.

"Yes. I make jewelry for a living."

"Really. Tell me about what you just made."

"It's a lariat with a large amber focal stone. I usually sell my stuff but for some reason, I decided to keep this one for myself." Juliet looked at the tea kettle and noticed the steam coming out of it. "It looks like the water is ready. What's the next step?"

"Want to try something different today?"

She looked doubtful.

"Okay. At least I think so."

"It's spruce tea. There's ascorbic acid in it."

Charles turned to the fire and dropped some fresh needles into the mugs he had set on the ground.

"Let me show you how to take the kettle off the fire."

With the fork-shaped stick, he pulled the suspended kettle toward him, wrapped a thick cloth around the handle, then poured the boiling water into their mugs.

"Let it steep awhile. It's more potent that way," he said, covering the mugs with a flat piece of wood.

Juliet decided this would be a good time to give Charles the orange she brought. From her leather bag, she removed the nylon liner containing the groceries and fished out one orange. She hung the bag with the rest of the groceries on a large branch next to the path that led home.

"I know you're getting Vitamin C in your tea but I thought you might like to have this sometime," she said, presenting the orange.

Charles' eyes lit up. "Thank you!"

He admired the orange for a minute, then put it into his pocket so he could more easily lift the wood off of the mugs and check the progress of the spruce tea. Declaring the infusion complete, he handed Juliet her mug.

She took a sip, involuntarily making a face.

"It's an acquired taste, Juliet."

"No, it's pretty good. I was just surprised at first because it's so unusual. It's amazing how great things taste out here."

Her shoulders were hunched up around her ears in an effort to stay warm. Despite the fire, the cold had caught up to her again.

"Would you like to use the blanket you brought over yesterday?"

"Thanks. That sounds like a good idea." Juliet fought back a convulsive shiver.

He returned with the blanket draped around his neck, then pulled a large log closer to the edge of the fire pit.

"Why don't we sit here, Juliet," he said, gesturing toward the log. "Let's eat this great big orange now, too."

Juliet moved to the log and let Charles lower the blanket onto her shoulders and over her back. They sat with their legs extended and their feet precariously near the flames. Charles took out the orange and began peeling away its skin, using his pocket knife. With each stab of the sharp blade, citrus oil spurted away from the sphere. Once entirely free of the peel, Charles broke off an orange segment and offered it to Juliet. She took it into her mouth and felt the sweetness burst open around her teeth.

Charles ate a piece, too. "Mmm. That... is... heaven."

Juliet laughed, delighted at his response.

"It is good. I love fresh food. If I lived on a farm, I'd eat fruits and vegetables right out of the field."

"It's a lot of work to farm," he said.

"My aunt and uncle lived on one in Indiana," she replied. "We visited them every summer. I always wanted to go back for the harvest, but by then I was in school."

Charles held a single orange segment, shiny with juice where his knife had penetrated it. A tiny rivulet of liquid, glistening in the firelight, ran down the side of his large thumb. He brought the fruit to Juliet's lips. She took a bite from it, then lowered her eyes. He waited until she looked up again, then put the remainder into his mouth. They both turned to stare into the fire.

"Tell me more about that necklace you made, Juliet."

"Well, I'm actually wearing it right now."

"Can I see it?

The soft magenta sweater and the push-up bra had been forgotten. But just now, too late, she remembered. Out here in the woods, next to a man whose warmth was so close, Juliet became suddenly self-conscious and embarrassed, realizing she would have to present the jewelry to him in the same manner she had at Cohort's. There was no way around it, so she removed the blanket and rested it on the log. She stood and slowly loosened her scarf, unbuttoned her coat, and pulled the shearling back off her shoulders.

Charles sprung up from his position beside her on the log. She saw his pupils dilate with pleasure. And why not? He had only seen her bundled in a coat and scarf during their encounters. Charles moved his hand close to her throat, indicating that he would like to inspect the necklace.

"May I?" he asked.

Juliet nodded.

He touched the right side of the lariat where it lay on her collar bone and took it gently into his hand. Twisting one of the smooth stones between two of his fingers, he followed each consecutive stone down the lariat between her breasts, until he reached the amber at the very end. He held it there, rubbing its smooth surface between his thumb and his forefinger. Juliet felt the warm back of his hand resting on her chest.

"Cognac Succinate," Charles said softly. "It's a beautiful work of art, Juliet."

He released the necklace but did not step back. She could feel his breath on her face. Finally, they both turned again toward the fire.

Charles spoke first.

"I sit by these coals and look up at the sky for hours every night. It puts things in perspective. I realize how short life is. How insignificant we are on Earth. The universe wants us to feel everything and experience as much of life as possible."

He looked away from the fire and back at her. "I want to sample it all, Juliet. I don't want any of it to get away."

Like a streaming comet, Juliet felt her spirit soar through the sky in a blaze of intensity. She was so close to something tantalizing; fervent; potent. Instead, she clawed at her coat, pulling it back up over her shoulders. Her fingers clumsily worked the buttons. Her tangled scarf dangled lopsidedly to one side. She had spent a lifetime avoiding vulnerable, intangible moments like this. It was what she knew how to do best.

"I'm sorry. I have to go."

# RESIN

Juliet stumbled down the homeward path, grabbing the nylon bag of groceries off the branch as she passed.

Charles watched her disappear into the woods. He glanced at Juliet's leather bag where it glowed in the firelight on the rock where she had left it, then walked slowly back to his cottage.

A childhood fear resurfaced. Slowly and irretrievably, higher and higher, the roller coaster pulled Juliet up and over its steep rails. She sat tense and frozen on the slippery seat. Below her, everything shrank in size. Before and behind her, others fell into silent anticipation while she reeled between exhilaration and fear—desperate to get off the ride but, aware she had relinquished control. There would be no turning back.

The cart could jump the track, and during its fathomless plunge, she would be aware of every second of her fall, including the last one.

Or, the strap that was so securely fastened around her lap could snap, and with a violent motion, she would fly unfettered, landing in a crumbled mass, amid strangers.

Another possibility? She would enjoy the ride. She would feel wild; euphoric; free. Her long silky hair would blow all around her face. On the smooth seat, her body would glide from one side of the cart to the other. She would laugh and scream and feel incredibly alive.

Friday arrived. As scheduled, Skillman returned from his trip to Florida. Throughout the next week, Juliet kept busy phoning friends, practicing her cello, planning her next jewelry project. With discipline, all thoughts of Charles Westfall were banished. Life's order was restored.

She had been unfaithful to Skillman only once, over a decade ago. The guilty sting freshened with each recollection. Just like the cliché, it did not mean anything, but at the time, it seemed important to experience an affair because she worried her capacity for passion had died. It had been so long since she had felt the sensation. For just a few hours on that reckless night, Pandora's Box opened and she found the answer.

He was a stranger; someone she met at a jewelry trade show. She and Rachel had flown to Atlanta together for the event, booking separate rooms, a few doors from one another to allow Rachel extra space for Cohort's Gallery related paraphernalia. If she suspected anything about Juliet's liaison, she'd never revealed it.

Juliet's misstep began with playful banter during the first day of the show. Cognizant of the sexual charge between them and savvy to the man's clever sales techniques, she was nevertheless astounded at how swiftly she succumbed to his overtures, especially after limited familiarity. They took advantage of the celebratory confusion of the farewell reception and escaped to his hotel room.

The experience was a sumptuous frenzy of physicality that left her feeling exquisitely raw the next day. Alive. That one time had sustained her.

Juliet's car kept her warm as she drove down the bleak side streets on her way to Thursday night's Royce Art Center board meeting. At the stop sign, a solitary dog-walker, bundled stiff with layers against the cold, stamped his feet impatiently where he'd paused as a hedge against her failure to stop. She gestured him across. He tucked his neck back into his shoulders and rushed in front of her, too cold for further eye contact. Even the dog declined an opportunity to sniff at a yellow patch once they reached the other side of the road.

Set back from the street, on top of a picturesque hill, stood one of several Royce family mansions. This magnificent Victorian housed the Art Center. Juliet pictured herself here in the summer months, seated on a wicker rocking chair on the gleaming white porch. She'd look out over cool blue hydrangea nestled between heavy bursts of vibrant rhododendron blossoms. Steps away, enormous hostas and Black-eyed Susans would fill the gardens that bordered the lush green lawns.

On this winter night, Juliet drove up the long driveway to find glittering strings of tiny white lights wrapped artfully around each of the porch's columns. Navigating to the back of the estate, she parked in the spot between the cars of Susan Jones and Tanzy Lynch. Tanzy's vanity plate read MKITBRF.

Down the hill to her left was a tiny frozen pond. Someone had recently shoveled off the snow for ice skating. During summers long ago, her son Jonus had thrown rock after rock into that water, waiting for his mother to finish some now forgotten work at the Center. After intermittent years of casual involvement with the organization, she recently committed to more significant responsibility, becoming the newest of ten board members.

Juliet kept her hand on the outside of her car and carefully slid one foot in front of the other until she reached the Center steps, then rattled the latch, and opened the back door.

"There she is!"

In the warmth of the big kitchen, Susan Jones greeted Juliet with a quick hug.

"Hi, Susan!" Juliet looked around the room. "Hello, Tanzy. I'm sorry I'm a bit late."

Tanzy glanced over at her while wiping up the counter.

"Don't worry about it, Juliet. Everyone just got here a minute ago, anyway. Susan and I are almost done with these refreshments. Would you mind taking this tray in?"

As president of the board, Tanzy was all business.

Juliet hung her coat on the old brass wall hook, then joined Susan at the counter where she was handed a large tray of cheese and crackers. Pushing open the swinging wooden door with her hip, Juliet held it for Susan and Tanzy. Platters in hand, the three women walked together through the gallery and down the short hall toward the loud chatter of the meeting room.

Tanzy called the meeting to order.

"As you are well aware, the date of our major benefit is rapidly approaching so tonight I'd like to focus on the details surrounding this event. Let's start first with an update from our new administrative assistant, Susan, and then move onto committee reports."

As Susan briefed the group, Juliet looked around the large table. All the women were married, with the exception of recently divorced Lydia Randall-Sikes, now simply Lydia Randall. Her transformation from married to single fascinated Juliet. Lydia's hair invariably appeared freshly cut and blown out; the colors of her make-up reflected the latest trends; her clothing was flattering but conveyed authority. Although she knew the other women claimed to pity her for being alone, Juliet envied Lydia's new energy. It was rare to spot her idling around town anymore. She was fully employed and lacked the discretionary time for visits to the Claret Cafe or other local gathering places. And what of her love life, Juliet wondered. Did she have one? Lydia was undeniably attractive, but she was well over fifty.

"And now, let's hear about the progress of the entertainment portion of the gala."

Tanzy's reference to entertainment brought Juliet's mind back to the meeting.

"Juliet?"

"Yes. Thanks Tanzy." Juliet consulted her notepad.

"I've contacted the harpist and confirmed she will play near the entrance from 7:00–8:00 while the guests arrive. The pianist will play until 10:30. For $100 more in advance, he'll play until the end of the benefit, regardless of the time. And, as you know, in addition to those two professionals, I'm going to play Le Cygne, also known as The Swan, from Camile

Saint-Saens' Carnival of the Animals. It'll be a little comic relief."

Her humor earned a chuckle from everyone except Tanzy.

"Juliet, we know you will be magnificent and very much look forward to hearing you play. Thank you for your update."

Tanzy closed her leather embossed folio and folded her manicured hands over it.

"There is one more detail which I'd like to share with the board before we close for this evening," she continued. "Allied Machine Corporation's unexpected financial crisis means we can no longer rely on their generous annual support. We are facing a dramatic drop in funding. I am afraid there are some very difficult challenges ahead. If we don't bring in enough from the gala, the long term future of the Center is uncertain."

Susan's head shot up from her note taking. She needed her job.

Tanzy had more to say. "It is absolutely imperative that we do all we can to ensure a good turnout. I also need every one of you to encourage potential new donors to give expansively. Let's plan to meet again at this same time the first Tuesday after the event so we can more accurately assess our situation. Now, if there are no further comments or questions, I'd like to call this meeting adjourned."

On Saturday morning, Juliet walked down Chestnut Street and approached Glennie Callandra's home. She was reminded of how much she admired the old bungalow style residence. The stone porch pillars contrasted prettily against the carmine red house. Snow covered the bushes around the foundation and the garden that Juliet knew would be crowded with bright flowers in just a few months. She had spent countless hours kneeling next to Glennie in the black dirt, dividing hostas with a precise shovel stab, or scrutinizing the difference between a valuable perennial and a weed.

Glennie had returned from England Thursday afternoon. Because she knew Peter loved to entertain, she had already whipped up a Saturday evening gathering of their friends. She hoped to please her husband and counter the damage done from her long absence.

Juliet promised she would help prepare for the party. She rang the bell at the weathered oak door of Twenty Chestnut Street.

"Come on in!" she heard Glennie yell.

"It's just me!" Juliet opened the door and took off her boots, adding them to others on the mat in the foyer. She slid down the polished wood hallway to the kitchen.

"Hello, gorgeous! Let me hug you!" Glennie wrapped her long arms around Juliet. "It's good to be home again. I loved

India but there's nothing like good friends and modern conveniences."

"Oh, Glennie, I missed you. I'm so proud of you and your journey." Juliet affectionately tousled the woman's curls.

"It was quite a journey, wasn't it? I can't believe I actually had the nerve to go, after thinking about it forever."

"You were very brave."

"I feel different in some ways, but mostly a better version of who I was before I left. Does that make sense?"

Juliet nodded.

"I adored that ashram but I knew I couldn't stay forever."

"How was Peter when you got home?" asked Juliet.

"A little distant. What man wouldn't be if his wife abandoned him for two months with no phone calls? I think he's warming up again, though. I want this to be a new start for us. I'm doing everything I can to make it work. He probably has to go on some kind of journey himself, but I'm not sure what direction that would take."

"A physical journey or an emotional one?" inquired Juliet.

"We'll see. I don't really know. He suddenly seems strangely young to me."

"Hmm." While contemplating this statement, Juliet noticed Glennie's hand. "Wow, you're even wearing your wedding ring again. You must be serious. I haven't worn mine since I was pregnant with Deirdre."

Juliet held her left hand out in front of her.

"I know, I know. But I have to try everything. Peter hasn't even noticed."

Suddenly slapping the table with the palm of her hand, Glennie quickly changed gears.

"Goddess! We have so much catching up to do but I'm crazy behind getting this party ready. You really are saving the day!"

"I can't believe you're hosting a dinner so soon after your trip," Juliet said, tying an apron around her waist.

"It's the new me. I want to focus more on the home front."

"Ah, a domestic diva."

"We'll see about that. I'm going to try to get stuff done in advance so tonight I can at least appear relaxed. Only you will know the blood, sweat, and tears behind it all. I hope I can still stand up by the time seven o'clock rolls around."

Glennie's hair was comically asymmetrical, as if she had spent the night in a headstand position; something entirely possible for an accomplished yogini like her. Next week, she would resume her job as lead yoga instructor at The Sanctuary on Concord Street. Juliet occasionally dropped in on a class but lacked the commitment to become a devotee like her friend.

"You know what you always tell me, Glennie. Just breathe. In...Out. In...Out."

Juliet made a dramatic show of puffing out her belly with each breath.

"Very funny. Would you mind rinsing those beans in the colander and snapping off the ends for me?"

"Only if I can make myself a cup of tea first. Want one?" Juliet asked as she took the kettle from the stove and filled it with water.

"Yes, please. Constant Comment. Peter drank all of my Earl Grey. Sorry!"

The mention of bergamot flavored tea elicited thoughts of Charles. Although Glennie would never reveal a confidence, Juliet opted not to divulge her secret just yet.

The two women labored feverishly into early afternoon. With the evening's food prepared, they swept the floor, set the table, then shared a light lunch of hummus, toasted pita triangles, and raw vegetables.

"I guess I should go home and see how Skill is doing."

"Yes, you should. You're such a bad wife! I thank you and love you, though. Tell him it's my fault you were gone all day."

Glennie walked her friend down the hallway to the front door.

Juliet fastened the leather buttons of her coat, slipped on her gloves, then reached for the doorknob. Swiveling back toward Glennie, she teased, "Don't forget to breathe!"

She deftly dodged the dishtowel snapped in response and slipped out the back door.

Following the sidewalk down tree-lined Chestnut Street to Number Nine, Juliet lingered at the first bricks of the walkway leading to her own front door. So much history in this house, she thought, pushing the door open

Skillman called up the stairs to where Juliet was getting ready.

"Where's your big leather bag? I need it to carry the wine and your shoes to the Callandras."

Juliet opened her mouth to reply, then checked herself, remembering she had left the bag next to the fire pit at Charles' campsite.

"I'm not sure," she called out. "Just use a canvas one from the hall closet."

A few minutes later, Juliet slipped her hand through Skillman's arm as they made their way down the icy stairs at the front of their house. The night was still, except for the rushing sound of gas streetlights illuminating their way, and the crisp crunching noise of their feet smashing patches of frozen snow on the narrow sidewalk. In his right hand, Skillman swung the canvas bag containing the wine and Juliet's impractical high-heeled sandals.

"Who else have they invited, Jewels?"

"The Lynches, the Shaws, the Linds. And Lydia Randall."

"Won't Lydia feel a little awkward all by herself?" Skillman asked.

"I doubt Lydia has ever felt awkward in her life. She's been divorced for a year now, Skill. She's used to going places solo. I'm sure she'd like to find someone, but it's probably hard at our age."

Skillman squeezed Juliet's hand. "I know."

When they arrived at the Callandras', Juliet pressed the bell, then quickly pushed the door open. A rangy Peter Callandra strode toward them, his eyeglasses catching the glare of the light, his hand already extended to Skillman.

"Skillman! Juliet! Great to see you!"

Peter took their coats and led Skillman over to the bar while Juliet walked down the hall to where Glennie was working in the kitchen. She found her friend washing some pots at the sink, wearing a plaid apron over a short black velvet dress. Juliet planted a kiss on her cheek.

"Glennie, the house looks fantastic and you look even better."

"Thank you and thanks for coming early to help me out! Did you have a good afternoon with Skill?"

"Exhilarating."

The two women exchanged wry smiles.

Juliet was wearing her garnet drop earrings, a favorite of Glennie's.

"Someday, Juliet, I'm just going to rip those earrings out of your ears and take them for myself."

"You know they'd always look better on me," Juliet vamped.

They laughed, then Glennie quickly got down to business.

"Okay, here's what still has to be done. Take this lighter and light the candles in the bathroom, den, and living room. Let's leave the dining room candles unlit until we're just about to sit down."

Juliet took the lighter out of Glennie's hand and walked to the spacious living room. Skill and Peter were there, standing across from each other, holding their highball glasses at chest level, discussing the latest innovations in hybrid car design. Skill winked at Juliet. As she moved from candle to candle and the pillars warmed around their flames, the sweet fragrance of beeswax filled the room.

At exactly seven-thirty, the doorbell rang and Peter opened it to greet Tanzy and Mark Lynch.

The Shaws and Linds arrived a few minutes later, and by the time Lydia made her grand entrance, the Callandra home was vibrating with conversation and music, and rich with the aroma of good food. True to her plan, Glennie's preparation allowed her to spend time with the guests as soon as they arrived.

The old house felt inviting. Occasionally, a pop and hiss escaped from the depths of the stone fireplace. Soft light from jewel-toned Tiffany lamps on low side tables made the buffed leather couches glow. Just when the noise was at its peak, Glennie signaled Juliet to usher the guests into the dining room, then slipped into the kitchen.

The guests seated themselves around the table alternately by gender, with no one permitted to sit next to a spouse. Peter poured the wine liberally, and for the next hour, the focus was on drinking, laughter, and the enjoyment of superb culinary talent. When Glennie got up to clear a few plates, the other women followed her lead.

Peter remained seated, twisting his mustache, deeply committed to pontification. After a while, Glennie returned, put her hands on his shoulders and waited for a pause in the conversation.

"Would you like to offer the men some brandy, Peter?"

As she motioned toward the snifters poised on the sideboard between the built-in bookshelves, the men pushed back their chairs.

These couples were no longer anxious about being cast in stereotypical roles. Right now, they all wanted to be where they would have the most fun. For the men, it was the dining room. For the women, it was definitely with the other women in the kitchen. Together, they scraped plates and covered leftovers, straining to be vigilant, tipsy from the wine.

"I'm so lucky to have you guys!" Glennie opened her arms for a group hug in the kitchen.

Juliet caught the twinkle in Glennie's crinkly-eyed smile. The shorter women giggled beneath them. After they broke apart, Glennie prepared dessert on the only empty counter space, while the others loaded the dishwasher or washed and dried pots and pans.

"I heard there's a hermit living in the conservation land near those two vacant lots behind Birchwood Street," Tanzy Lynch proudly revealed.

Juliet looked down at her hands where they held the pot she was drying.

"Oh?" Susan Shaw's eye widened. "Where did you hear that?"

"I have my sources," Tanzy replied.

"Is that even legal?" asked Anna Lind.

"If he's handsome and single, I want to meet him!" Lydia Randall spoke with a hint of a slur.

# RESIN

The women laughed, but Juliet forced her lips to stretch over her teeth to mimic the appropriate emotion, suddenly feeling a world apart from the others.

Glennie lifted the tray, heavy with goblets filled with chocolate mousse.

"Dessert is ready, ladies. Let's get back in there before your men drink so much brandy you have to carry them home!

The start of the Dyson Health Center's mid-winter term brought a schedule change to Juliet. Hot yoga was no longer offered on Wednesdays so she swam instead. Afterward, she walked toward the train stop, mindful that she had no particular plans for the day. She felt emotionally brittle because of it. The bitter cold did not help her mood.

Back in Winston, she noticed Rachel crouched on the floor of Cohort's large display window, deftly repositioning an iridescent vase. Juliet managed a weak smile and wave, then hurried by.

Further down Concord Street, she paused for just a moment to peer over the edge of the bridge. Thousands of beige and gray pebbles lined the banks. Occasionally, a large rock blocked the flow of clear water, causing bubbles to gurgle around it. She realized she had never really noticed this stream before. Standing there, staring down at the water, Juliet wondered how many other things in life she had missed.

Despite the cold, she didn't want to go home. There were too many reminders about the tedium of her days that exacerbated emotions she wished to avoid. Juliet could conjure up only one option for delay and that was to retrieve her leather bag from Charles' campsite. It was a necessary task she had avoided.

She left the bridge and turned onto the path where it opened up behind the gnarled trunk of the big oak tree. The trail was difficult to detect once again; snow had thawed and frozen over it numerous times since her last passage. She was anxious about being observed, but she quickly plunged through the woods anyway, having faith she would eventually find her bearings. If she hugged the stream, she knew she would arrive at the general vicinity of the campsite.

The morning seemed to have grown exponentially colder with each hour. Despite the impediment of trees, the wind came at her in stiff gusts and her skin burned red from the sting of it. She cursed her decision to pack only a flimsy ear band instead of a warm hat to cover her wet hair.

Eventually, she smelled the campfire and saw Charles Westfall crouched by the stream, dipping a red cloth in and out of the water. He would be surprised by her arrival, and she relished the thought of feeling in control, even for a moment.

"Charles," Juliet said quietly.

He looked up, his face open.

"Juliet! I was just thinking about you."

He stood, wrung out the cloth, placed it on top of a rock, then strode toward her.

She was determined to maintain her composure but could feel strength leave her knees.

"I...I'm here because...because I forgot my leather bag and...and...I need it."

Her senses alternately sharpened and blurred, strobe-like."

"Okay," he said, drawing out the word, "I kept it in the cottage so it wouldn't get wet."

He scanned Juliet's face, then turned and walked slowly toward the cottage. Juliet followed, deliberately keeping a few paces between them. When they reached the cottage, Charles turned to her and offered a gentle smile.

"I'll be right back with it."

He lifted the doorway flap, then disappeared inside.

The dazzling sun was in sharp contrast to the sub-zero mid-morning temperature. Squeezing her arms around her torso, Juliet jumped up and down a few times to offset her shivering, again cursing her foolish decision to leave the health club with wet hair.

Charles came out of the cottage.

"Here you go, Juliet," he said, handing the bag over to her.

"Thanks."

"You look cold."

"I'm freezing," she chattered, visibly shaking.

As much as she wanted to stop, she could not control the involuntary reaction to loss of body heat.

Charles stood in front of her, very still; his arms at his sides, his legs slightly apart, seemingly unaffected by the cold. Without a hat, his ears had turned bright pink. The puffy down-filled jacket he wore was unsnapped. Juliet noted the pattern in the wavy tortoise shell button at the top of his wool shirt. Wisps of white chest hairs curled over the round collar of the thermal layer underneath.

He held his head erect. She had to bend her neck to look up at him. Bright green eyes focused on her.

Finally, she broke away from his gaze and looked down. First at the snow between them, then over to his boots and the dangling upper laces. He had left them untied, stuffing the pant legs into the boots to keep the hems free of snow. Her eyes traveled up his calves and thighs. The thick blue jeans were cut loose but did not disguise the smooth plane of muscle beneath fabric. The brown jacket again. His neck. His face. His eyes.

Juliet took a step forward—instantly enveloped in the warmth of Charles Westfall. She felt his mouth press into her hair, then his warm, moist breath on her cheek. He pulled open his coat and wrapped her inside, conjoining them in a feather cocoon. The shivering continued.

"Juliet, come inside and dry your hair."

He took off his coat and wrapped it around her, guiding her to the opening and underneath the heavy flap. Juliet smelled the scent of cloves in the folds of his coat as she settled into the down warmth. She stood stiffly on the wood floor just inside the entrance, while Charles knelt down at the fire and blew great gusts into the rising flames. The lodge soon glowed with golden light and heat.

"Please, sit down," he called over to her.

Juliet walked obediently to where Charles motioned and sat on one of the stools close to the fire. Standing behind her, he removed her ear band, careful not to catch any rogue hairs. Stuffing the band into his pocket, he held her skull firmly with both hands, then moved his fingers in a circular motion, massaging her scalp. Charles deftly separated the long wet strands of blond and gray hair, pulling them apart and arranging them over her back. Applying a little pressure on her shoulders, he encouraged her to turn her torso sideways, directing the heat of the fire onto her hair. Over her legs, he spread the worn wool blanket she had given him.

Juliet's body temperature was slowly returning to normal. Huddled in the enormous down coat, her eyes focused on the floor until she heard a beautiful, lyrical sound. At the other side of the room, Charles blew into the mouthpiece of a silver flute. She smiled for the first time, then turned back again toward the fire so her hair would dry.

"Can you stay for lunch?" he asked, when he finished the song.

"I'd love to. Thanks."

Lentil soup was cooking in a pot suspended over the fire pit outside. Every so often, Charles excused himself and left the cottage to check on its progress. Juliet took advantage of this solitary time to consider where she was and what was happening to her. She swiveled around on the stump and examined her surroundings.

He had enough supplies to last for several months, stored neatly on the branch and twine shelves he had constructed. There were beans, onions, cans of vegetables and fruits, and jars of dehydrated foods. She saw glass containers of rice, quinoa, and millet. There was a large tin marked "OATS" on one shelf. Three colored glass jars were filled with whole almonds, walnuts and Brazil nuts. Juliet's mouth watered at the sight of familiar foods she loved.

The next time Charles left to check the soup's progress, she rose and looked around for some utensils, intending to help with meal preparation. She found a set of four forks, knives and spoons stored on end in a battered old can. Next to that were four enameled tin bowls of various sizes and colors, stacked upside down. When she discovered neatly folded Indian print fabric squares on the shelf below, she smiled, imagining Charles using napkins for his solitary meals deep in the woods. Juliet quickly set the table and waited for him to return.

With nothing to busy herself, her chest grew suddenly tight and her head felt light. Despite the cool temperature, her underarms were damp. She realized she was at the mercy of a man who was clearly eccentric, possibly dangerous and certainly capable of getting whatever he wanted. Added to that was the impropriety of being alone with someone who others would prejudge and condemn. Not a soul knew where she was. Everything in Juliet's rational mind warned her to leave at that moment, but the increasingly loud crunch of boots on snow signaled Charles' imminent arrival. When the giant man pulled aside the flap and stood in front of her, she made a snap decision to let her intuition guide her. She would trust the overwhelming sense that he meant no harm. She would give into this tremendous attraction and let the momentum pull her to a place she had never been.

"I see you've located my pantry."

He set the pot of hot lentil soup onto the table.

"I didn't want you to do all the work. I hope you don't think I was being nosy."

"Of course not. I appreciate your help."

He lit the wick of an oil lamp and set it a little off-center between the two of them; so they could have a clear view of one another. They sat down at opposite ends of the rough table, balancing on their tree stump seats.

Like a real couple, thought Juliet, suppressing a giggle.

"Was it a good joke?" asked Charles.

"I was just thinking of how we looked, eating out here in the woods with napkins and soft lighting. But it is lovely and the soup smells delicious," she quickly added. "Thanks so much for sharing it with me."

"The honor is mine, Juliet."

He removed his napkin from the table, unfolded it once onto his lap and placed the remaining fold close to his waist. Toward the end of their meal, when his soup bowl was nearly empty, Charles tilted it away and deftly spooned the last few bites into his mouth. He brought his napkin to his lips, dabbed at the corners and patted over his beard to capture any stray morsels.

It felt perfectly natural to simply sit across from him in silence. Although Juliet was curious, it seemed rude to ask personal questions; best to wait for Charles to offer information when he was ready.

"Would you excuse me, please?" He stood, walked over to his shelves and returned with a metal tub into which he collected their bowls and spoons.

"This is my sink," he said, winking at her.

"You use the water from the stream to wash your dishes?"

"Only after I boil it. I mainly use it to wash clothes. I purified the well water for a while but it's safe. I tested it."

"Would you like some help washing?"

He set the tub onto the table.

"Next time we'll do it together, Juliet. You will come again, won't you?"

"I'll try."

Juliet stood, looking around for her things.

Charles bent to retrieve her headband which he had left to dry on a rock by the fire. She put out her hand to take it, but he slipped it onto her head, lifting her hair, adjusting it over her ears. The headband was extra warm where Charles' large hands pressed it firmly in place. When he tilted her head up toward him, she looked into his eyes and noted the line of gold circling each pupil. With reflexive anticipation, her lips parted and eyelids lowered. Charles gently released her, moved to the doorway, and held aside the flap.

Juliet felt her face redden. Had she actually thought he would kiss her? Had she intended to let him?

Together, they moved out of the cottage and into the light of the campsite where the wind had picked up again. When a stray hair blew over Juliet's face and caught in her lips, Charles took it between his thumb and finger and wove it back amongst the others, then stroked her cheek.

"There will be another time for us, Juliet."

As if in a trance, she turned and walked down the icy path toward home. She had forgotten her leather bag again.

There was perfect tension in the hair of the cello bow. Juliet nestled it in the valley of the rosin block and rubbed the little box back and forth, and back and forth again, in short, brisk strokes. She hiked up her bathrobe and spread her legs, positioning the smooth wood of the cello between them, feeling pressure where the edges rested on the inside of each thigh.

Soon, eighth and quarter notes warmed the long, thick strings. Rosin dust gathered on the surface beneath them. The steady tempo and fluctuating pressure of her touch caused the cello bridge to relent almost imperceptibly.

She and the instrument combined forces and moved through Le Cygne. The woman swaying, eyes closed, breath quickening; the cello vibrating in a low voice with an occasional lilt. At the last note, Juliet let the bow fall from her hand to the floor. She brushed a strand of hair from her face, leaned back on her chair and released a deep sigh.

Then, she began to cry.

Juliet dragged a rocking chair over to the window, sat on the hard seat and rocked in silence. It was clear that whatever she had once felt for Skillman had perished. Perched at this crossroads, she was terrified of growing into an old woman whose sole ecstasy in life might be the taste of a restaurant's decadent dessert. An appetite for carnal knowledge as a ripe adult, so different than her youthful sexual encounters, gnawed at her. It was a pull as strong as the call to give birth she had felt decades ago.

At the mirror the next morning, she scrutinized her naked body. Yes, she was older; and yes, she looked older. Her breasts hung low, her stomach had rounded, and the skin of her thighs was dull and loose. Did it matter? Her body was a thing to treasure, to explore and to experience for her own pleasure, as well as a man's. It was time she became the seeker, as well as the sought. She would see, touch, smell, taste—because she must.

Downstairs in the kitchen, Juliet picked up a speckled banana and brought it to her nose, closing her eyes and inhaling the sweet scent. She ran her finger along the side of the fruit, broke off the top and peeled it away. With the first bite, saliva flowed as her taste buds reacted to the tender pulp. Her new intention was to slow her actions, savor everything around her, and become greedy for sensation. She smiled at the impracticality of truly and fully experiencing all of life this way. She could not pause every moment to sniff, or taste, or feel, or hear whatever she encountered, but she would find a way to take in all she could.

Charles spent some time assembling a simple, yet elegant chair from sturdy birch branches gathered over several days. After securing the final twig with twine, he positioned the chair next to the fire and turned to attempt a trial sitting. Comfortable enough, he decided, and certainly more comfortable than the tree stumps, logs and rocks he had been using. He stretched his long legs out in front of him, brought his hands behind his head and laced his fingers together.

This was how Juliet found him when she appeared at the entrance to Charles' campsite the next day.

"You look like a king," Juliet said.

"I feel like a king when I see you."

He stood to greet her.

She leaned over and patted the top of the newly assembled furniture.

"Did you make this chair?"

He nodded.

"I started building it last night."

"It's beautiful. I've never seen anything like it. How did you know how to design it strong enough to hold your weight?"

"I have an engineer's mind."

"Ah. At last, I get to learn something about you."

"What else do you want to know?" asked Charles.

She hesitated.

"I'm not sure. In a way, I feel as though I already know you."

Juliet crouched down and absently guided a twig through some embers glowing at the edge of the fire.

"I'm glad you feel that way, Juliet."

"Want to know anything about me?" Juliet said, looking quickly up at Charles.

"Only what you want to tell me," he replied.

"I think I'll leave things the way they are."

Juliet stood again. Side by side, they stared at the fire.

"Would you like me to make a chair for you?" Charles asked.

"Could you? That would be wonderful!"

"I have quite a few branches left but we'll have to gather some more."

He took her hand and led her into the woods behind the cottage. Bending down, he picked up a birch branch about one inch in diameter.

"This is the size we'll need."

They spent the next hour collecting branches and depositing them into a center pile. Charles occasionally pointed out an animal track or alerted Juliet to a bird call he thought would interest her.

Later, next to the fire, Juliet admired Charles' dexterity as he secured twigs together to construct her chair. Veins and tendons rose and fell on the back of his capable hands. His fingernails were packed with dirt, soot and sap, but for the most part, they were clean hands, and they were making something for her. She longed to feel them again in her hair. On her face. On her uncovered skin.

In slightly over an hour, Charles stood the fully assembled chair upright next to Juliet.

"Now, let's see if it works. Are you ready to take a trial run?" he asked, smiling.

"I'm almost afraid to sit in it. I'll feel horrible if I ruin your masterpiece."

Charles patted the seat of the chair with his hand.

Juliet lowered herself carefully onto the chair, surprised at how sturdy it felt. She looked up at Charles. With bright sun behind him, the features of his face were a blur, but she could easily discern his bulk as he leaned over and rested his arms on the sides of her chair.

"I can't imagine a prettier sight than you in this chair."

She met the green eyes, then her neck loosened and her chin moved toward his face. As she lowered her eyelids, she felt his lips on hers, soft and warm. He kissed her lightly, pulled back to scan her face, saw her smile with pleasure, then returned to part her lips.

Charles Westfall drew her in at a pace that was maddeningly slow. It took all her resolve to resist grabbing his head and pulling it toward her for the next deep kiss she craved.

"I don't know what to say or do. I'm totally out of my depth here," Juliet confessed.

Charles knelt on the snow next to her.

"Juliet, you don't need to do or say anything. It's only necessary that you be. It's taken me a lifetime to understand."

She lowered her head.

"I'm married, Charles."

"I figured you were," he said. "Do you want to talk about it?"

Her eyes returned to his face.

"No. I don't even want to think about it. I do want you to know one thing, though."

She looked back at her gloved-covered hands resting on the outside of her thighs, then pushed them along the length of her legs, holding her knees together.

"I want you to know that I'm not a bad person. I want you to know that I don't want to hurt my husband or my family. I just want to feel alive."

Her heart raced as she struggled to control the pace of her breath.

"Juliet, you are an incredibly beautiful and extraordinarily intelligent woman. I want to share whatever you want to share with me. You're in control here."

"I feel like I'm walking down a new road and I don't know the way, but it's a path I want to take," she said.

They sat side by side in their matching chairs, holding hands, gazing into the fire, until they both heard the unmistakable sound of Juliet's stomach growling, and burst out laughing.

"I guess I'm not a very good host! I don't even have lunch prepared yet," Charles said. "It looks like today might be a good day to open one of those cans in the pantry."

He helped Juliet to her feet.

"Would you like to choose from my vast supply of gourmet offerings?"

"I'd be honored," she replied, then walked toward the cottage and pulled aside the entry flap.

Inside, sunlight filtered through the thick glass of the old windows and lit the pitted ocher walls. Juliet was giddy, even giggly; barely competent to make a decision between chili or ravioli. Finally she grabbed the chili, a can opener, a pot, and a large spoon she found on the bottom shelf, then hurried back outside into the radiant day.

"I see you managed to find everything."

A pleased Charles looked up at her from where he tended the fire. "Would you like some carrots with that chili?"

"I didn't see any in the cottage."

"I haven't shown you my root cellar yet," Charles called out as he walked away from the fire.

He kicked some snow away, heaved a large rock to the side, then lifted up a broad piece of wood. Down on his hands and knees, he rummaged around in the previously covered pit.

"Voila!" His hand emerged, grasping two large carrots.

"Bravo!" Juliet applauded his ingenuity.

After they finished lunch, and the pot and dishes were washed and put away, Charles and Juliet prepared to say good-bye. Charles put his arms around her waist and rested his interlocked hands on the small of her back.

"Will I see you tomorrow?" he asked.

Juliet enjoyed the sensation of being held by a strong, tall man, so different in shape and affect from Skillman.

"Yes, I can probably be here around ten."

"Then it'll be a real lunch date, and this time, I'll be prepared," Charles laughed.

He pulled Juliet a little closer, took her face into his hands and kissed her.

She felt herself collapsing and pulled back to take a deep breath.

He released her slowly. "Until tomorrow, then."

Taking her hand in his, he walked to the edge of the clearing, brushed her cheek, then handed her the leather bag.

Part way down the path, she turned and saw him through the trees, still standing in the same place. Juliet tore off her glove and brought her hand to her face, savoring the hint of his scent on her skin.

Although the general layout of Winston was familiar to Charles from his boyhood visits, the town had changed considerably. The stores were different. The people were different. Winston had become an exclusive community, and an excluding one as well. Status cars vied for parking spots. Designer handbags hung from the arms of smartly dressed women. Ethnic minorities of questionable immigration status hurried about completing errands for their cash paying employers.

Charles easily located the old landmark of Blersch's Market. At its entrance, he stood aside to open the glass door for a young woman. She hesitated, then swept through the entrance, suspicious of his chivalry. Charles knew his unkempt appearance and imposing physique caused a stir in this upscale town. He could have selected a less busy time of day for shopping but with only a short list of things to pick up, he set about the task.

Near the door, he grabbed a basket from the top of a stack and walked down the middle aisle toward the meat department. There, the butcher wrapped up two small steaks for him. In the produce section, he selected a bag of potatoes, a few small beets and some dried fruit. At the checkout line, he tossed two individual packets of dark chocolate into the basket.

Mr. Blersch emerged from his back office and began to straighten the already uniform magazine display at an adjacent checkout stand.

"Did you find everything you needed?" he asked Charles.

"Yes. Thanks very much." Charles gently set his items on the conveyor belt.

The young cashier stiffened when she noticed the black dirt under his fingernails. Cognizant her boss was monitoring both her and her customer, she busied herself ringing up the small purchase.

"That will be $24.82, please."

Charles dug deep into his pocket and counted out the exact amount, all in coins. In the line forming behind him, a few customers exchanged exasperated glances.

"Do you mind if I bag this?" Charles asked the clerk.

"No, that's fine. Thanks." She continued sorting the coins splayed in front of her.

Charles walked over to the end of the counter, grabbed a paper bag, snapped it open, and began arranging the food inside. Mr. Blersch changed his position to stand beside the cashier.

"Your receipt, sir," the clerk said, holding out her hand.

"Thank you," he replied, then nodded congenially to the manager as well.

The store was quiet as he walked over the sawdust covered linoleum, then through the doorway.

"Who do you think that was?" one of the customers questioned the crowd in general as she unpacked her cart.

"I have no idea. He seemed very polite, though," someone said.

"I really don't think we need people like that shopping here," another woman offered. "It's disgusting." She directed her comment to Mr. Blersch, who was already halfway down the aisle, but still within earshot.

Skillman opened his attaché case, reached inside and pulled out several legal-sized manila folders, spreading them over the kitchen tabletop.

"Juliet, you wouldn't believe what a pain in the neck this case has become. Apparently, there are some family members who are balking at the merger terms, even though we spent months trying to prevent this very thing from happening."

"That's horrible, Skill."

"Yes, it sure is. It means I have to fly to Omaha and spend two weeks holding hands until they can reach an agreement."

"Two weeks?"

"I'm sorry, Jewels. Thank goodness it won't conflict with your performance. The whole thing will be resolved one way or another before then. I promise."

Skill took his wife in his arms.

"I know how much you like your time alone, so hopefully this will be a nice little vacation from your husband."

Juliet patted Skillman's back, but looked over his shoulder and through the window into the direction of the Town Forest.

That night in bed, she slept restlessly, juggling a jumble of thoughts. She reminded herself that she was too old to be impetuous; nevertheless, she was tired of evaluating her actions in terms of others, always living with a mature obligation to the collective good. She wasn't sure anyone cared about the right things she did but felt certain they would care about the wrong. Her husband would board a 10am flight out of Boston. She would be alone for two weeks.

Skillman bent over Juliet and kissed her gently. "I'm heading out now, Jewels."

"Oh, is it seven already? Good luck, Skill. I know you'll get them all straightened out."

She propped herself up.

"I'll miss you," he said.

"I'll miss you too."

Juliet balanced on her elbows, listening. She monitored his footsteps on the stairs, then in the kitchen. She heard the car drive away down the alley.

With new energy, she sprang out of bed, put on a fresh set of sheets, showered, styled her hair, checked her email, and baked a dozen muffins.

Outside, the plink-plink of melting icicles suspended from the porch roof dripped onto the thawing muddy snow.

It was time to visit Charles Westfall. On impulse, she raced up the creaky back stairs and into her bedroom, heading straight to the delicate glass perfume bottle on the dark wood dresser. Anointing her wrists with the spicy scent, she pressed both onto the pulse points behind her ears.

In the hallway, she adjusted the fit of the outdated coat previously destined for charity.

The kitchen burst with the heavenly scent of freshly baked walnut-oat muffins which Juliet had already wrapped in foil and packed into her leather bag. She grabbed it from the kitchen counter, closed the door behind her and walked down the empty alley.

Just as she was about to veer off the gravel road and enter the path, a woman called her name.

"Good morning, Juliet!"

Claire Houghton stood on her porch, waving.

"Good morning! How are you?" Juliet responded, waving in return.

It would be rude to walk by the elderly woman and not stop for a short chat, so she trudged over the chunks of dirty snow at the end of the driveway and walked up to the porch where Claire stood wrapped in her full length mink, a few inches of flannel nightgown visible beneath the hem.

"What a beautiful morning, Juliet. Busy day ahead?" Claire ventured.

"It's gorgeous. I'm going to work out and I may lunch with a friend," she replied.

"That sounds nice. How are Skillman and the kids doing?"

Claire was clearly in the mood to chat, so Juliet set her bag down on the bottom porch step and shared a family update. The elderly woman had watched all of the children in the neighborhood grow up and had been a kind and generous presence during those years. Everyone who knew Claire ached for her when her husband passed away. They seemed so much in love, even at the end of their long lives.

After about fifteen minutes of small talk, Juliet searched for an opportunity to say goodbye.

"Be careful walking through those woods, Juliet. There's a crazy rumor that a hermit is living there! Can you believe such silly talk would spread in this town? I guess people don't have enough on their minds already. If you ask me, we should just leave the poor man alone—if it's even true there is a man in there. After all, it's not like he's hurting anyone."

"I promise I'll be careful. You be careful too, Claire!"

Juliet picked up her bag and walked back down the driveway and across the slushy street.

On the path to the campsite, she considered the hermit-in-the-woods rumor, wondering how it had spread. She hadn't mentioned a word to anyone and would not mention this to Charles now. She didn't want to be one who brought sadness into the perfect world he had created.

It was nearly 10:30 when she arrived at the clearing. Charles sat by the fire, his chair pushed close to the edge. Her empty chair was next to his.

"Good Morning, Charles," Juliet greeted him, a trill in her voice.

"Juliet! Good morning!"

Charles rose from his chair and walked toward her with his great stride.

"I thought you might have changed your mind today."

"I'm sorry I'm a bit late. There's an elderly neighbor who lives across the street from the path and I got caught up in a chat. I just couldn't rush by."

"That sounds very much like you."

Charles ran his hands through her hair, then held the back of her head.

Juliet smiled, enjoying his green eyes, the pink in his cheeks, the curly white of his beard, and the invitation on his lips. She felt her breath quicken.

"Let me take your bag, Juliet."

"I brought some muffins to have with our lunch. I made them this morning."

Charles brought the bag to his face and inhaled.

"What a delicious scent. We're going to have a feast!"

He hung the bag on a sturdy tree branch.

"Would you like some of the same kind of tea I made for you on your first visit?"

Charles poured water into the tin cup then handed it to her.

They settled comfortably in their chairs in front of the fire.

"I was a little afraid the first time I saw you, you know," Juliet said, with a sideways glance.

"Why is that?"

"Well, first of all, I was surprised to find you in these woods. I couldn't believe you actually intended to live here. And, in a tent no less! I was just going along in my ho-hum day and then you appeared out of nowhere."

"And?"

"And, it's sort of given me a different perspective. I was feeling a bit stuck. Meeting you has loosened up something that needed adjusting."

"That sounds like a good thing, Juliet."

"It is good, and I am happy that I'm here. It's just that I don't really know *what* I'm doing here."

"Do you have to know?" Charles studied her face.

Reflexively shy under scrutiny, she encouraged herself to try a bold approach. After a long pause, she took a deep breath, then looked directly into Charles' eyes.

"I don't even know where to begin, Charles. I've been married so long."

He gave her an encouraging look.

Juliet summoned the nerve to elaborate.

"I've been unhappy for a long time. I couldn't quite figure out why. It appears I have an almost perfect life," Juliet sighed.

They both looked down at the fire.

Juliet continued. I can't believe I'm telling you all this. I don't know why, but I want to. Will you promise to stop me if I start to say more than you want to hear?"

Charles sat up in his chair and leaned toward her.

"Juliet, please. Don't worry about what you're saying. I want to hear as much as you want to tell me. I'm honored."

She took another deep breath. Instead of returning her gaze to the fire and continuing her confessional in a less intimate way, she forced herself to focus on Charles' open face.

"Time is slipping away and there are so many things I still want to do. And feel. I want to travel to places where I've dreamed of going. I want to speak to people I don't even know yet. I want to touch things that are foreign to me."

She sighed.

"I wish I wasn't afraid to do these things by myself, but I have to admit, I am. That's one of the ways I disappoint myself. At fifty-six, you'd think I'd finally be brave enough to venture out on my own."

Charles took her hand in his.

"Juliet, I can't know how you feel but I think I understand your desire. You've met your responsibilities and fulfilled your obligations. You've done all the right things in life but you still want more. The meat no longer satisfies—you need to break open the bones and suck out the marrow."

Juliet stifled a giggle.

Charles raised his eyebrows. "What?"

"The part about the marrow. I'm a vegetarian."

Charles threw his head back, laughing.

"Well, I guess I'll have to think up a better analogy!"

"No, Charles that was fabulous advice. I'm only just beginning to explore these issues."

They smiled at each other, appreciating good conversation.

"Here's a question only you can answer." He grinned. "I bought two steaks for our lunch, so what should I cook for you now?"

"I can't believe I'm saying this, but I'd like to try one of those steaks. I'm a nutritional, not a philosophical vegetarian. I don't remember when I last ate a steak. It'll be a virginal experience for my taste buds!"

"If you're sure..."

"Yes, I'd love a slab of meat."

"I'm still stuck on 'virginal experience.'" Charles winked at her, as he moved to ready the cooking fire.

The unseasonably warm day eventually brought hard rain, but fortunately only after the meal had been fully cooked over the fire pit. Juliet marveled at Charles' skill in food preparation. Along with steak, he braised beets and potatoes. They ate their hearty lunch at the wood table, enjoying the contentment of full bellies while in the cozy shelter of the cottage.

Juliet set her fork on the edge of her plate, pushed her hair back from her face with both hands, and looked at Charles.

"My husband is out of town for the next two weeks.

Charles watched her face.

"I'd like to visit you more often," she said. "If I wouldn't be imposing."

"Come as often as you like and for as long as you like."

Juliet considered the double entendre. After all, sex seemed to be the logical progression of this liaison. The only question was whether Juliet wanted to progress to that point.

The rain stopped.

"I should probably get going. I have to do a few errands this afternoon," she said.

"I'll miss you." Charles' eyes moved to her mouth and back up to her eyes again. He took her hand and slowly raised it to his lips, kissing her palm and taking in the scent of her skin with a deep, slow breath. Juliet fought to calm the beating of her heart. She wasn't ready to lose control.

Juliet stood and looked around for her leather bag.

"I promise I'll be here again soon."

Juliet floated down Concord Street sporting a Mona Lisa smile. At the window of Cohort's Gallery, she paused to admire the painting she loved, oblivious to Rachel waving to her from inside the store.

Finally, Rachel opened the door and stepped out onto the sidewalk next to Juliet and asked, "Can I help you ma'am?"

"No thank you, I'm just..."

Juliet shook herself out of her trance.

"Oh, Rachel! God, what a space case!"

She leaned over and hugged her friend.

Rachel returned the hug, then held Juliet at arm's length, scrutinizing her face.

"You smell like a girl scout who just left her campfire!"

"I guess I should take this old coat to the cleaner."

Juliet looked down and brushed a few rogue pine needles off her sleeve.

"You're fine. But you sure were lost in my window art."

"I love this painting. There's something about it that makes me want to take it home and hang it on my bedroom wall."

"No one has made an offer yet. You could be first."

"Okay, I think I'm back on earth again. We both know how much it costs."

"You have a point. Well, I've got to get back to the shop. Can you come in and visit?"

Rachel held the door open.

"No, sorry. There are some things I still need to get done."

"Don't make me wait too long for my next Juliet fix!" Rachel laughed.

There were no errands. She wanted only to savor this special mood. Having abandoned her original plan to work out at the Dyson Center, she continued strolling down the street. At The Sheepe Shoppe, a window display of colorful yarns nestled in baskets caught her eye. She opened the door and went in.

The earthy scent of wool and natural dyes transported her back to an era when she frequented yarn stores. Fashioning numerous sweaters for her children as they grew through their many sizes, had made Juliet an excellent knitter. Skillman joked about the fact that she had never made him a sweater. She wasn't sure why that particular project had not come to fruition. It would have made him immensely happy to have her spend hours working on something for him. He would have worn the finished product with pride.

Next to the entrance, two dozen skeins of moss green wool were neatly stacked on an antique table. She pulled one chunky strand out from the center of the top hank, noting a subtle thread of soft sage running through dark moss. The same color as Charles' eyes. She could knit a sweater for him. Spring would arrive soon and he would need something less heavy than his down jacket. There would be ample time to make progress on the project while Skillman was away. She could finish the balance of it at the campsite during visits with Charles. Finding a pattern and corresponding needles from the collection she had at home would be simple. With an educated guess about the amount she'd need, Juliet counted out sixteen skeins of the same dye lot, then carried them over to the register.

The stout clerk spread the skeins over the counter, checking the dye lot numbers against one another.

"Looks like you have an ambitious project in mind. Sixteen skeins?" she confirmed, looking at Juliet above her glasses frames.

"Yes. That's right."

"Do you need any needles or other notions today?"

"No, I'm all set. Thank you."

Juliet handed the clerk her leather bag to fill.

At the jingle of bells, they both looked toward the door where Susan Shaw walked in. Her friend spotted her right away.

"Juliet! I'm not surprised to run into you here!"

Juliet smiled as Susan walked toward her.

"She is hands down the most talented woman in Winston, you know," she gushed to the clerk.

"Oh, Susan. You're very kind," Juliet said.

She was anxious to verify that the skeins were packed into her bag, but didn't want to risk attracting Susan's attention to her project. With Skillman away, Juliet had allowed herself to relax in the false security his absence had created.

"I told you Gil wants me to take up a hobby, so today, I decided my new hobby would be knitting!"

Susan dubiously surveyed the perimeter of the store from the safety of the center counter.

"I have absolutely no idea where to start, though."

Juliet took the receipt from the clerk, then quickly swung the bag behind her back, hiding the purchase, and her sap and soot covered hands and fingernails.

The clerk had already turned her attention to Susan.

"Well, you've certainly came to the right place. I'd be more than happy to get you started with a beginner project. We even have a knitting group that meets here on Fridays so you can get help along the way."

She guided the novice toward the nearest shelf of yarns.

"Good luck with your new hobby, Susan," Juliet called, moving toward the exit.

Susan looked surprised that her friend was leaving so abruptly.

"All right. Well, bye then."

Just before Juliet reached the door, Susan called out to her again.

"Hey! Lydia has the week off so we're having lunch at Claret's on Thursday. Want to join us?"

"Thursday?" Juliet hesitated, consumed with her desire to spend the week with Charles. "I think things are clear for that. What time?"

"High noon. See you then!"

"Thanks, Susan."

Juliet left the store, dangling bells on the door jingling in her wake. Outside, she took a deep breath of fresh air, reversed her direction on Concord Street and resumed her walk toward home. She would not allow herself to see Charles a second time today. She didn't want to appear too eager or risk upsetting the balance of whatever was developing between them.

At the curve where the bridge and Concord Street merged, Juliet noticed an empty police car parked at the entrance to the path. It was a routine parking spot but she wondered how long it would take for the police to eventually venture into the woods and explore the veracity of the town rumor.

Back in her kitchen, she poured water into the tea kettle then set it on the burner. She raced downstairs to beat the boil, rummaging through boxes, searching for the musty sweater patterns and worn leather knitting needle case, until the kettle whistle screamed.

With a steaming mug and project materials at hand, she sat down and perused the patterns. Selecting an easy cable design, Juliet gathered needles and yarn, quickly casting on one hundred and forty-seven stitches; the first step in creating a sweater for Charles Westfall. For several hours, the only sound in the kitchen was the soft click-click of wooden needle against needle as Juliet persisted with her labor, even when the room became too dark for her to see.

Later that evening, Juliet balanced a glass of Merlot on the bathtub ledge, slid into the steaming water, and extended her legs upward onto the wall above the faucet. Removing the marker from the middle of a novel, she settled in for a good read. After several chapters, she allowed the paperback to fall to the bathroom floor, then looked down through the water's blue tint at her flesh.

This decades-old body had served her well: magnificent in carrying and birthing three children with no medical or pharmaceutical aid; powerful in hiking the granite peaks of the White Mountains of New Hampshire; graceful in swimming the width of a glass-smooth Walden Pond. It been steadfast through all these years, yet Juliet was not confident she had mined the depths of her physicality.

Over the last few years, her libido had diminished to only a memory, presumably in response to shifting menopausal hormones. How was it then, that tonight, six years after her last period, desire summoned? She arched her back at this new craving—spiritual, earthy, wanton, and uninhibited. She yearned to release the corpus and simply feel without awareness. Flesh as flesh itself. Bolts that had fastened tight to contain a potentially insatiable appetite were loosening.

Sunlight streamed through the sparkling clean window where the curtain had been left open the night before. Stretching languidly across the king-sized bed, Juliet opened her eyes and smiled, an image of Charles fresh in her mind. Like a teenager full of butterflies, she longed to explore first time emotions and sensations, again.

She had virtually no biographical facts about Charles, the man for whom she was about to jeopardize everything. This she felt she knew: he was brilliant, kind, industrious, inventive, creative, practical, witty, educated, well-traveled and sensitive. All of that, and he had not had a proper shower in a very long time.

Juliet rose from her bed, smoothing brocade and fluffing stuffed pillow shams, then left to turn on the shower.

She recalled the many times she had tried to spin her marriage to convince herself that life with Skill in the town of Winston was enough. She acknowledged that an affair with Charles was emphatically and obviously wrong on so many levels, she had a hard time counting them.

Massaging conditioner into her hair, she let hot water pelt her lower back. What would she gain from a liaison with another man? A chance at last to taste an emotional rainbow? Without Skillman, and the steamer trunk of marital baggage they dragged behind them, she would be free to explore her sexuality. A relationship with Charles might open up new paths she had never dared imagine, but all would pay the price for her pleasure. Why did she have to hurt her loved ones to truly love herself?

Pulling the warm towel off the heated rack, she dried herself, massaged organic coconut oil into her skin, brushed her teeth with the electric toothbrush, and then dried her hair. She stepped into soft corduroy jeans, and chose a butter-yellow silk shirt and an ivory sweater to wear over it.

At the kitchen window, the thermometer read twenty-two degrees.

The air smelled crisp and clean as she made her way down the uneven gravel alley, then along the path to the clearing. Juliet would see Charles this morning, for just an hour or so, allowing her feelings to guide future action.

The campsite was empty when she arrived. There was no fire burning in the pit.

"Charles?" she called out softly.

Juliet walked up to the cottage entrance, surprised to find the wrinkled canvas flap replaced by a wood door.

"Charles?" she called out again.

The door creaked open and Charles stepped out, wiping his mouth with a cloth.

"Good morning, beautiful! You caught me brushing my teeth."

"I just noticed the new door and was getting ready to knock."

"You, my lovely, can simply walk in whenever you fancy."

Charles beckoned her with arms that were strong and warm around her.

"It's too cold out here for you today. Let's go inside and have some acorn brew."

"Acorn brew?" She laughed.

"You'll love it!"

Charles held the door open, then followed her into the cottage.

"I harvested some acorns from that old oak over by the stream about a month ago. The brew is called Raccahout. Tastes more like hot chocolate. It's my humble effort."

Charles handed a mug to Juliet.

"Smells nice." A skeptical expression contradicted her words.

"Take a small sip and see what you think. I've sweetened it with a little molasses."

Juliet sampled it. "It's different. Actually, pretty good. It tastes a lot less strong than I thought it would."

"Acorns could feed much of the world, Juliet. Native Californians relied on them for at least half of their food source."

"Are you kidding? Did they just drink this brew all of the time?"

"No, they converted their supply into flour also." He was eager to educate her. "The oak at my campsite is Quercus Macrocarpa, a bur oak. Its acorns have a relatively low bitter tannin but I also shelled and boiled them. We could grind them and make acorn chips, crackers or even muffins. Of course, they'd never be as good as the muffins you make."

"Thank you." Juliet curtsied toward Charles.

He stroked her hair. "Oaks don't produce acorns until they're fifty years old. Sometimes the best things come later in life, Juliet."

. . . . . . . .

Juliet called Glennie later that same morning, hoping to catch her before she left to teach class at the Yoga Sanctuary.

"Hey, it's me," Juliet announced.

"Hi. You sound subdued."

"I'm just really relaxed because Skill is out of town for two weeks."

"Bliss. I could go for some of that right now, too."

"Has the ashram glow worn off already?"

"Kind of. You know, the 21st century is no place for women like us."

"You're right. But, I can't figure out where else we'd fit. Maybe with the Amazons?"

"Very funny. At least we're tall enough. So, what's going on with you?" Glennie detected anxiety in Juliet. They rarely kept secrets from each other.

"A bunch of stuff. You know. Don't you have your class this morning?"

"No, today is the new term. My class starts at four now. I've been lounging around all morning. Do you want me to come over?" asked Glennie.

"Could you please?"

"Put the kettle on and I'll be there before it boils."

Juliet hung up the phone, carried the tea kettle to the sink and filled it with water. She was desperate for feedback and advice. Was it right to drag anyone else into her metamorphosis?

Glennie let herself in at the front door, walked back to the kitchen where Juliet was unloading the dishwasher, and hung her coat on the back of a chair. Glennie's red hair had its characteristic asymmetrical slept-in look. Wrinkled pajamas previously hidden under the long coat proved how quickly she had rushed over.

"It's not fair of you to look so beautiful in the morning."

"I did have a chance to shower and do my hair. And, I've already been out," Juliet replied.

She set steaming mugs on the table, then they both sat down, propping their feet up on extra chairs.

"Okay, go," Glennie said, scanning Juliet's face.

Juliet lifted her index finger to her mouth and gnawed a little on the nail while Glennie arched one eyebrow in anticipation.

"I think I'm falling in love, Glennie."

"What? What are you talking about? Did you meet somebody?"

"Yes. But, it's all so unbelievably complicated." Juliet's voice broke as she brought her other hand to her face and rubbed her temples.

"Start at the beginning. Do you want a hug first?"

"Yes."

Glennie got up and leaned over to embrace Juliet, then took her friend's hands into hers and held them while she sat back down.

Juliet inhaled and exhaled with force.

"I don't know how it all started. It's so bizarre, Glennie. I know I'm going to sound like a freak."

"Oh, Juliet, you're not a freak. Tell me what is happening."

"Do you remember at your dinner party when Tanzy talked about that hermit guy living in the conservation land next to the vacant lots?"

"The rumor?" Glennie looked blankly at Juliet.

"It's him."

"What do you mean, 'It's him'? What about him?"

"He's not a hermit, Glennie. He's an incredibly beautiful and gifted man who's camping on that land."

"Are you serious? Juliet! He could be crazy!" Glennie looked at her with alarm.

"No, he's not crazy but I might be," Juliet responded with a laugh, which swiftly became a sob.

"Oh my god. Okay, I really need you to start over."

Juliet looked down at their hands clasped together.

"Glennie, I know we trust each other completely, but I feel like I need to ask you first of all, if you can keep this a secret, and second of all, if you want me to burden you with the details?"

Juliet's eyes brimmed with tears.

"I'm here for you, Juliet. Whatever you need."

"I didn't go looking for him. He just kind of arrived in my life."

Glennie nodded, encouraging Juliet to continue.

"He visited Winston as a boy. His uncle built a cottage in the woods. I really don't know many details about his past. I only see who he is now."

Juliet paused, looking up at the ceiling.

"He's the most incredible person I've ever met. I'm both at peace and excited when I'm with him. He's gentle and kind and he knows everything about living in the woods."

"But, why does he live in the woods?"

"I don't know. He says he likes to and that he's done the same kind of thing all over the world."

"And you believe him?"

"I know it doesn't seem plausible. If you knew him, you'd see he's authentic. He has a very calm and humble personality but I can tell he's quite an accomplished human being."

"What about Skill? Does he suspect anything?"

"Oh God, Glennie. You know he's so good to me. I feel horrible about this. That's why I need to talk to you!"

Glennie stood to grab a few tissues from the box on the top of the refrigerator, then handed them to Juliet.

She said, "This has been brewing for a long time."

"I know. I love Skill so much but I think I'll need another kind of man for what I still want to feel. It just seems unfair to hurt someone who would literally die for me."

Juliet burst into convulsive sobs.

Glennie scooted her chair next to Juliet's and put her arm around her friend's heaving shoulders. For a few minutes, the rhythmic ticking of the clock on the wall was the only other sound.

"I can't live this way anymore. I'm beginning to feel like I'm an outsider watching myself go through the motions of my own life. Do you know what I mean?" She looked over at Glennie.

"Juliet, you know I love you more than anything, right?"

"And I love you, too."

"I will always listen to whatever you have to tell me and I will never, ever judge you."

"Thank you," whimpered Juliet, folding a limp tissue into an increasingly smaller square.

"But Juliet, I can't tell you what I think you should do this time. Only you can decide. And, my dear sweet friend, you do have a decision to make."

After Glennie left, Juliet forced herself to be industrious, spending a few hours at her workshop developing prototypes for new earring designs, practicing her cello, loading laundry into the washer and dryer. She took the yarn basket out and set to work again on Charles' sweater. Her wooden knitting needles tapped a muffled sound. The waning rays of the afternoon sun illuminated the metal cable needle where it rested on the kitchen table. When Juliet held the sweater up to gauge her progress and visualized it stretched over Charles' chest, she buried her face in the soft green wool.

Eventually, she ran out of ways to keep busy. A clear day became a dark night.

She watched the moon rise through the black glass of the bathroom window. She had already soaked in the porcelain tub for almost an hour. Between her toes, she twisted the faucet to the left, adding more hot water to the bath. Occasionally, the radiator clanged as heat moved up from the basement and made its way through the old house.

When she finally released the drain, the water level gradually lowered until there was no liquid left and all that remained was pink flesh. The bath had done its magic; loosening her joints, relaxing her muscles, and releasing a peaceful energy. Juliet stepped out of the tub and rubbed her towel over the fogged mirror, impassively contemplating her flushed reflection. The wall behind her was cool. She leaned her shoulders and bottom against the smooth, slick tiles. Slowly, back and forth, she slid across them.

On the counter, droplets of water rolled down the sides of a bottle of sandalwood-scented oil. Juliet reached for it and poured a generous amount into her hands, warming the liquid between them. Starting with her breasts, she spread the oil over herself, slowly, rhythmically. She hugged her arms across her chest and distributed the oil, working it into the softness of her belly and her back, then spreading it down the sides of her thighs. She massaged the oil into her feet and calves and worked her way up the front of her legs. There she lingered, a potent scent left on her hand.

Turning off the bathroom light, Juliet walked into her dark bedroom. The moon had moved high in the sky. Squares of cool light fell through the window panes and stretched across the expanse of the room. She removed silk long underwear from her dresser drawer and laid it on top of her bedspread, then collected a thick wool sweater and her softest blue jeans from the closet shelf. On her marriage bed, she propped opened her leather bag and dropped the clothes and a fleece jacket inside, slipped the supple strap over her naked shoulder, then walked downstairs.

At the very back of the hallway closet, she rummaged around for the fluffy texture of the full length fur coat, impulsively purchased at an estate sale twenty years ago. Too ostentatious to wear in public, Juliet had instead draped it over her children when she read to them on cold winter evenings. Tonight, she stuffed mittens and a hat into its pockets, then pulled on the heavy coat, adjusting the collar and fastening the closures. The smooth satin lining felt delicious over bare skin. She slipped into the leather boots warming by the radiator, hoisted her bag over her shoulder, then opened the door to the alleyway and stepped outside.

The windows of most of the houses were dark; it was nearly eleven o'clock on a weeknight and many of her neighbors had early commitments. Bright moonlight dominated the alley where sharply defined shadows of bare trees pointed across the yards she passed. Few stars were visible. It was bitter cold and quiet, except for the crunch of her boots on the frozen snow.

Down the alley, Juliet stepped carefully across the shine of icy patches until she reached the entry to the path. She stopped a few steps into it, closed her eyes and inhaled the scent of pine, letting the crisp air fill her lungs, then resumed her journey down the path toward the clearing.

The fire pit was black but the cottage's frost-etched windows glowed. In the darkness, she heard magical soft notes from a flute. She walked up to the door and pushed it open.

Charles sat in his chair by the white fire. He looked up, surprised, as Juliet entered the room. Without looking away from her face, he laid the silver flute on the ground next to him, then rose from his chair and moved slowly toward her. Neither spoke. Juliet unfastened the heavy fur coat and let it fall off her shoulders. Charles stopped where he was and sucked in his breath as he watched her enjoy the luxurious cascade down her smooth skin. The coat landed in a heap on the old wood floor.

In an instant, they were in each other's arms. Charles' warm hands were everywhere; his soft lips sampling the well-primed woman so eager to give, and, receive.

Juliet woke early the next morning to a vison of bright sunlit-stencil designs on the faded cottage walls. As she recalled the passion in the dark the night before, her lips squeezed into an impish smile. Around her waist was a long muscled arm, and at its end, a broad hand positioned protectively over her pearl belly. She angled her face back up toward Charles.

Resting his head on the flesh of his free arm, he returned her gaze, his green eyes bright and clear. Instantly, her heart thrilled, rekindling the warmth in her groin.

"Good morning," he murmured.

"Good morning to you, Charles Westfall."

He removed his hand from her waist and stroked her cheek with the back of his fingers.

"Would you like some breakfast?"

"Yes. You," she answered.

She turned her body toward him, throwing her leg over his and wedging her foot between his calves. Into Charles' chest and neck she burrowed, inhaling the scent of his skin, passing her parted lips across his flesh. A sudden ferocity of conquest propelled her on their rustic bed. She wanted to devour him—a novel concept for her—but flames in the fireplace had dwindled to embers and Charles could not neglect the hearth. He tucked the furs snug around her, then withdrew to feed a few logs to the coals, promising to return.

This was Juliet's first opportunity to behold the naked Charles from afar, exposed for her pleasure at last. The man was a slab of muscle, every inch pulsing with vigor. His feet were wide but dexterous, his calves covered with hair, his thighs long, his buttocks tight. As he knelt to tend the fire, she took in the view of his broad shoulders, noting a scattering of freckles.

Sensing her gaze, he turned and smiled. A soft moan escaped from her. This was the man she wanted.

After they were spent, and tears came to Juliet's eyes, Charles held her tight. "What are you feeling, Juliet?"

She lifted her wet face to him. "I'm happy and sad at the same time."

He absently rubbed the velvet indentation at the bottom of her spine. "We're together now, Juliet."

When Charles left their bed, he moved Juliet's boots next to the fire. She finally found the fortitude to leave the luxury of their nest, walked to the fireplace, and slipped her feet into those toasty boots. Thousands of goose bumps quickly gave texture to the rest of her skin.

Now it was Charles' turn to admire her. He took her in unabridged, his eyes resting on each inch, as if she was Venus herself. Juliet turned slowly around to tease him, leaning over from her waist to pick up her fur coat, then wrapping it tightly around her.

They spent the morning as new lovers do, turning mundane tasks into private moments of intimacy. When they passed each other in the tiny cottage, they stopped to exchange sweet, slow kisses. Charles dressed in jeans. The tail of his flannel shirt hung beneath the hem of his battered down vest. Juliet wore the warm fur coat over her nakedness. Charles cooked a pot of coarse oatmeal, adding bits of chopped dates and almonds to it as it cooled. Juliet set two places for them at the table.

There were numerous morning chores to complete, but Charles would not allow Juliet to help. He intended for her to have a pampered and relaxed day. She pulled her fur coat closer and settled into blissful reverie in her chair next to the fire. Giving no thought to Skillman, or the rest of her family either, Juliet mulled over the possibility of a future with Charles, temporarily losing herself in the fantasy. Perhaps she and Charles could stay here for a while but later move into a house. Or, maybe they would travel to another state to launch a novel bohemian adventure.

She avoided the unpleasant fact that she knew virtually nothing about his past. It was her stubborn taboo about revealing her own circumstances that led to this distressing lack of knowledge about his. Other lovers would have preceded her. She quickly turned away from the thought. She was the lover now.

Charles returned, handed Juliet a cup of tea, then knelt next to her on the granite hearth. He stoked the crumbling logs.

"Do you enjoy reading, Juliet?"

"It's one of my favorite things, especially in bed at night."

"Did you miss it last night?"

They exchanged conspiratorial smiles.

"I was an English major," she said.

"Oh? What books did you like?"

"Madame Bovary, Scarlet and Black, Anna Karenina, anything by Charles Dickens, and my very favorite would be Shakespeare."

"Did your parents like Shakespeare?"

"Because of my name?"

He nodded.

"Here's the story. My mother didn't like to read but she liked to travel. One of her favorite places was Paris. Since I was born in July, she named me after the French name for that month. But, hardly anyone could pronounce Juillet, so my parents changed it to Juliet."

Interesting. Both names are beautiful. I always liked the month of July because it starts the second half of the year. It's a chance for a fresh start."

"What a great thought. How about you, Charles? Do you like books?"

"I do, but I keep returning to the ancient classics. The Odyssey, Beowolf, all of Dante and The Aeneid."

"Impressive!" Juliet commented. "I was amazed to learn the Odyssey was originally recited, not read."

Charles began to speak another language.

"Oh my god," Juliet sat bolt upright. "Don't tell me you know ancient Greek?"

"And Latin. It was required at my school. We spent quite a lot of time in front of the classroom reciting dactylic hexameter," he chuckled.

A follow-up question about his school location was in order, but Juliet checked herself. An examination of facts and reality would end their paradise.

The new couple spent the morning in light conversation, revealing the special and personal things they loved most about the world, until Juliet suddenly stiffened.

"Charles, do you know what time it is?"

"It's probably close to noon but if you wait a minute, I'll go check the sun. Is everything okay?" he asked, moving toward the doorway.

"I forgot I promised to meet some friends for lunch. If it's almost twelve, I'll have to head right over there and I won't have time to go home and clean up first."

Juliet held her arms in front of her, looking down at herself. It was clear she felt living outside for one night and morning made her unfit for any other human companionship.

"Hold on a second then. Let me check."

"Juliet immediately grabbed her leather bag, pulled out the clothes she had packed, then hastily dressed.

Charles returned. "It's noon, Juliet."

She was already zipping her fleece jacket and putting on her mittens.

"I'm so sorry I have to rush off this way, Charles. I'll be back soon, though!"

Juliet reached up to kiss him, then raced out the door. Charles followed her outside and watched her run down the trail toward town.

Behind the glass of the stone clock tower face, the black hands read twelve-twenty. Because the traffic light in front of City Hall was taking forever to turn red, Juliet bounded over piles of dirty snow and ran across the street anyway. Breathing heavily, she pulled open the door at the entrance to the Cafe and excused her way through the packed foyer of women waiting for available tables. She was confident Susan had made a reservation and was already seated.

Beads of sweat formed on her forehead as she scanned the room for Susan and Lydia. Juliet maneuvered between the packed tables, burning with awareness at how disheveled she must appear. The brief look of alarm on Susan's face confirmed her concern, but her friend extended her arms to pull Juliet into a hug anyway. The two of them could pretend there was nothing unusual about her today. She braced herself for less tact from Lydia. When the other woman simply smiled, Juliet slid into her seat and took a quick sip from the glass of wine waiting at her place.

"I'm sorry I'm late! I was busy working on a necklace and lost all track of time." She didn't enjoy lying.

"We were just seated ourselves because it's so busy, Juliet," Susan said. "I hope you don't mind I already ordered you that glass of Merlot!" Her smile was a little too bright.

"Thanks, Susan. I really need something to drink after the way I rushed over here."

"Cell phone?" Lydia asked.

Juliet shrugged. "It's not charged. I never use it."

"I don't know how you do it." Susan shook her head. "Gil must call or text me ten times a day to do one thing or another for him."

"Exactly!" laughed Juliet, searching for her old, familiar social rhythm.

"You could have driven here." Lydia said, staring intently at Juliet.

Susan quickly intervened. "You must be getting really excited about your performance coming up!"

"I am. I've been practicing a lot. I hope I don't screw up."

Susan patted her on the hand. "You'll do fine."

The waitress appeared, ready to take their orders. After she left, the heat of Lydia's scrutiny became overwhelming.

"Is everything okay?" Juliet asked her.

"It's this new dry eye medicine. I actually have to remind myself to blink, it works so well. I'm probably staring like a crazy woman."

"Oh!" Susan burst out, "Speaking of crazy, that reminds me! Remember at Glennie's party when Tanzy said she heard about a hermit living in the Town Forest?" Both women looked at Juliet.

"Yes?" she responded with a feigned lack of curiosity.

"Well, her cousin works for the police department and he says they've actually charged that man with vagrancy, along with a few other things." Susan continued. "And, this hermit guy is supposed to be unbelievably attractive, in a very rough sort of way!" Susan leaned back in her chair, basking in her contribution.

"Mmm," Lydia purred. "I'm up for something different like that!"

Juliet brought her wine glass to her lips and crinkled her eyes to avoid commenting.

Mercifully, their waitress returned, setting plates of artfully prepared food on their table. Juliet quickly seized the opportunity to change the subject, and to her relief, they chatted amicably about other topics until the meal's end.

It was then she realized she had no money on her, having neglected to prepare for lunch the night before.

"Darn! I left the house so quickly, I forgot my money."

Susan came to her rescue once more.

"How about if I pay this time and you can just take me out again next week? I know where to find you."

"Thanks so much, Susan. I definitely owe you one."

"No cell phone, no wallet, no brain." Lydia teased Juliet.

"I promise I'll turn over a new leaf. Soon." Juliet laughed as she stood to leave. "Right now I need to get back to my workbench. See you later, ladies." Juliet leaned over and kissed them both on the cheek, then made her way back through the crowded tables to the exit.

The two waved to Juliet as she passed them on the other side of the restaurant window.

"Phew!" She and Skillman must have been really busy," Lydia said, suggestively raising her eyebrows.

"What do you mean?"

"Couldn't you smell it all over her? I don't think she was working on jewelry this morning!" Lydia laughed.

"Really? I didn't notice that but I was kind of thinking she was letting herself go a bit. When I saw her a few days ago at the yarn store she was wearing some baggy old coat. She didn't wear any make-up then, either."

"*Something's* going on," mused Lydia.

"I just hope she's okay." Susan folded her napkin and placed it neatly on the table.

Lydia left right away, intent on day-off errands. Susan plucked a mint from a basket on the hostess stand and lingered, chatting with several women she knew. Tanzy Lynch emerged from the restroom and spotted her right away.

"Hello, Susan."

"Hi, Tanzy. Here for lunch?"

"Just finished. You probably didn't see us sitting in the back corner. I saw you with Lydia and Juliet."

"Isn't it nice to slow down and catch up with friends once in a while?" offered Susan.

"It is. You and Lydia must be busy, but I bet Juliet has a lot of time on her hands with Skillman gone for so long."

Susan looked startled but recovered quickly. "He really does his share of traveling."

"Mark told me the firm sent him to Omaha for two weeks. Not the best place during the winter, that's for sure." Tanzy shuddered at the image.

"No, I guess you're right about that. Well, I'd better get going, too. See you later, Tanzy."

Susan left the restaurant with a heavy heart. Juliet had not mentioned Skillman's absence, even though they had often taken advantage of his travels in the past. Last summer, the two friends took a spontaneous trip to Nantucket. At other times, they camped out on her over-sized couch, watching movies and eating popcorn. Apparently, Juliet was busy with something new in her life that she didn't want to share. It was rude to pry into a friend's personal affairs without being invited, so she would just have to wait patiently. Susan hoped she could reciprocate for the many times Juliet had helped her through difficult transitions. She resolved at the very least to protect Juliet and speak up in her defense, if that became necessary. If there were secrets, she would not pass along any, either.

Juliet paused in the middle of the Concord Street bridge as she followed the shorter street route home. Below, icy water rushed over a mash of decayed leaves lodged around shiny stones.

She surmised that the patrol car parked nearby a few days ago evidenced an official visit to Charles. He hadn't mentioned anything to her about it, though.

While checking her house before returning to the campsite, she listened to phone messages via speaker in order to further expedite her departure.

"Message received, 7:30am," the voice announced.

"Hi Jewels." It was Skillman. "Just checking in before I head over to the conference. You're probably in the shower so I'll try back later. Love you."

"Message received 10:00am."

"Darn, I missed you again. Well, I'm sure you're doing fine. The merger is a mess but it looks like we'll still stay on schedule. I'll try to email you. Bye for now."

"Message received 10:47am."

"Hi Juliet." This time it was Glennie. "Just wondering how your 'project' is going. Let me know if you need any help. Okay?"

Juliet ran up the kitchen staircase, two at a time. There on the floor of her room was the towel in a lump where she had dropped it the night before. How dramatically her life had changed from yesterday!

Opening bureau drawers and closet doors, she gathered a collection of her warmest clothes and carried them downstairs, unloading the pile onto the kitchen table. At the front closet, she dug out the old coat worn earlier in the week, then reached up to the top shelf and pulled down two canvas bags last used for a family trip to the beach. Juliet winced as she pushed the image of those innocent days aside. She returned to the kitchen to stuff one of the sturdy bags full of clothes, then bolted back upstairs to fetch her toothbrush and hairbrush from the bathroom. Back in the kitchen, she gathered Charles' partially completed sweater and placed it at the bottom of the remaining bag.

Juliet opened the refrigerator and bent over the door, surveying its contents. She had decided to contribute food to Charles' household to relieve his financial burden. Cash would flow as well, if that became necessary. Removing a carton of eggs and a few loose vegetables, she nestled them into the bag, on top of her knitting.

It was becoming easier to understand the simplicity of Charles Westfall's life. She pulled on her coat and with one hand on the doorknob, paused for a moment to contemplate other possible needs.

As she walked down the alley with two big canvas bags slung over her shoulders, she hoped neighbors would not find her demeanor completely out of the ordinary.

"Ah, you're back," Charles said, relieving Juliet of her heavy bags.

"I feel bad I had to rush off, Charles. I didn't want to leave you," she said, standing in front of him, her arms now dangling empty at her sides.

She was trembling, intentionally leaving herself open and vulnerable, reveling in an almost perverse pleasure of emotional risk. She pulled on his arms, burdened with the canvas bags, and led him toward the cottage.

"Let's go in right away," she said, pushing the door open.

Inside, Charles dropped the bags simultaneously onto the cottage floor. Intoxicated with desire, Juliet unzipped his jacket and pulled his shirt over his head, not wanting to waste a minute on buttons. Her neck arched back. Her breath moved hard and fast through open lips.

Wanting to witness and savor the power of her desire, Charles made her wait, but only briefly. At last, he put his arm under her knees and picked her up, reaching their bed in a few long strides. She tore off her sweater, desperate to feel his skin against hers. In seconds, they were together again. Juliet let all thoughts of the outside world fall onto the floor and rest on top of the tangle of their clothes.

Charles pointed to the bags set haphazardly on the floor. "What's in those, my little fox?"

Juliet nibbled playfully on his shoulder.

"I brought some warm clothes and also some food I knew would spoil in my refrigerator." It then occurred to her that she had not been invited to move in.

"I'm sorry. I shouldn't have assumed..."

Charles put his finger on her lips.

"I don't want you away from me for a minute. Come back into my arms."

That afternoon, he rearranged his shelves to accommodate Juliet's belongings. She would be a part of his life and his household. With that in mind, Charles began Juliet's practical instruction He showed her how to tend the hearth, explaining why he stored different varieties of wood. She learned that ash and white birch burn optimally when green, and that a heavier wood has a greater burning potential. She listened attentively as Charles explained the best way to create coals for cooking by starting with a softwood such as pine, then switching to a hardwood like oak. He shared all of the important details that would enhance their comfort in the cottage.

That night, after supper, Charles asked if she would like to wash herself.

"Honestly, I would. I'm trying not to think about it but I'm not used to feeling this way. Also, I'm worried I might offend you."

"Impossible. Washing is not just to clean, it's for survival. This afternoon when we spent all that time traipsing through the woods, your body was working hard. If you don't remove that sweat, you'll start to chill later tonight. It's so much easier to do a little nightly washing, than warm up after being chilled to the bone."

"Okay, you've convinced me. But I'm warning you, you'll have to stuff a sock in my mouth once I feel that cold water on my skin."

Charles' smile was charitable.

"I can tell I've missed something," she said.

"You'll see."

He disappeared out the door and returned with a large pot of steaming water.

"Oh, I get it!" she laughed.

"There's more. The water is hot now but that won't last. Do you see these stones next to the fire?"

Juliet nodded.

"They're soapstone, or steatite, which is incredibly dense. Soapstone absorbs and radiates heat."

"I never knew that." She marveled at the breadth of Charles' knowledge.

"I always warm a few of these up after supper to use at night. You probably didn't notice them tucked under the bed."

"You're right. I can't say I was thinking about that." Juliet smiled mischievously. "I thought it was just you keeping me warm."

Charles dipped into his pocket. "Dessert?"

He unwrapped one of the chocolates he bought earlier in the week and split it neatly into two pieces. "One for you." He held it near her lips and watched her slowly take it into her mouth. "And one for me."

"How can I wait for my bath, Charles Westfall?"

"You must. Like savoring chocolate, the sensations will be even more rewarding. We have so much to explore together, Juliet."

Charles collected an irregular shaped chamois and two small wooden bowls from one of the shelves. He dropped soapstones into the wooden bowls, dipped a tin mug into the steaming mother pot and transferred some of the water to the others.

"One of these bowls is for washing and the other for rinsing," he explained.

"Would you like to go first?"

The fire at her back was burning vigorously, so Juliet obeyed when Charles instructed her to remove all her clothing above her waist. He rung water from the chamois and moved closer.

"It's best to do one small area at a time. I'll work slowly so the chamois can reabsorb what the fire doesn't dry. First, your face."

Tenderly, he washed behind her ears, over her forehead, cheeks and chin, then around her neck. He took her hand and washed each finger carefully. It was impossible to get the black out from under the nails but the earthy origin of the dirt did not trouble Juliet. Charles made long, stroking swipes up her arm. When he reached her breasts, she closed her eyes. Such a large man with such a gentle touch. Charles reversed the process, thoroughly cleansing her from the toes up. It was hard to contain the bursting she felt inside, so she focused on the reward Charles had promised would follow this exercise in self-control. She wanted to live up to his expectations.

It was her turn. Dipping the chamois into the water and ringing out the excess liquid, Juliet stood on the tips of her toes and carefully washed the ears of the burly Charles Westfall. She delighted in this wonderful opportunity to get to know him in another, differently intimate manner. His bathing took longer because of his size but the time spent was a pleasure for them both. When she washed the bottom half of his body, he showed heroic restraint. With the ritual cleaning complete, she wrung out the chamois and emptied the water. The bowls sat undisturbed on the table until the morning sunlight danced around their smooth wooden rims.

Several days later, Juliet left the cottage to conduct another house check. It would have been a nice gesture to invite Charles to join her, but she didn't, and she was ashamed to acknowledge the many reasons why. For one thing, she didn't want anyone to suspect she was cheating on her husband. When is one possibly ready for that? But why not simply invite him into her home at night when it was dark and no one could see?

As she shuffled down the frozen alley, Juliet reviewed the exhibits of her personal history on display at Nine Chestnut Street: family photos, furniture choices, and an intimate kitchen nook that held countless memories. She was reticent to let Charles view the spectrum of her life. She wasn't ready to erase her past. Perhaps she was already too close to the end of life to start a new beginning.

At her kitchen counter, Juliet picked up the phone and played her voice messages. Skillman had called two more times. He would eventually abandon his effort to communicate, as Juliet anticipated. He was confident she would contact him when she was ready, or if anything was seriously amiss. Glennie, or one of their friends, would reach him on his cell phone if needed. This had always been the couple's unspoken agreement. Juliet liked her space and Skillman didn't want to risk annoying her by checking in too frequently.

In the dark study, she listened absently as her computer booted up the familiar chime. Before checking her incoming mail, she composed and sent a breezy, duplicitous hello to Skillman, who was not expected home for at least another week. He preferred to fly on weekends so she was confident he would not take a flight home before next Saturday. Because she had sent him the recent email, she knew he would not be hurt by a continued lack of contact. That's really all it took.

She returned to the main page. Scrolling down the headings of the various new emails, she deleted those she could ignore, then stopped at one marked URGENT and clicked the mouse.

From: Social Responsibility Committee

To: All Unitarian Universalist Fellowship of Winston members

During the "Joys and Concerns" portion of last Sunday's service, Frank Comtois brought to our attention the story of "Charlie," a man who lives in a non-traditional manner deep in the Town Forest. "Charlie" has recently been charged with vagrancy as well as a variety of other legal offenses by the Town of Winston. This is a social injustice taking place right in our own community.

As many of you know, the Social Responsibility Committee has adopted this man's cause. We believe a man who has chosen to live in Winston on unused land in a peaceful but non-compliant lifestyle, should be allowed do so, unmolested. Because he has chosen to live outside of our community norm in an unconventional construct, and because he is causing harm to no one, we feel strongly that he should not suffer harassment from our local authorities. To that end, following next Sunday's service, we ask that you consider signing a petition to pressure the Town of Winston to drop the charges currently levied against "Charlie." Copies of the petition will also be posted throughout the area and we ask you to encourage your friends and neighbors to sign them as soon as possible. A contingent from our Committee will present copies of this petition to the Mayor, the Chief of Police and the District Attorney at the conclusion of the signing. It is our sincere wish that this will have a positive effect on the outcome of this case and the life of an innocent man.

Yours in Peace,

Clint West

Chair, Social Responsibility Committee

Juliet's hand shook as she clicked "Print," then waited while the machine spit out the copy. She read the memo again, wondering if she should make Charles aware of his dubious celebrity status. It was just a matter of time before "welcoming" UU ambassadors wandered back into the woods to pay homage to him. Juliet did not want to be there when that occurred. She slipped the paper into the desk drawer.

Bookshelves lined the wall behind her. She turned to peruse the hundreds of titles neatly arranged on the shelves, then took down two: Thoreau's Walden and Shakespeare's Sonnets. Opening Walden, she flipped to "The Pond in Winter," examined a few pages, then slowly closed the leather cover and carried both books into the kitchen.

Juliet sat down at the familiar kitchen table. What exactly was she doing to her life? It was irresponsible of her to avoid examining potential outcomes of her behavior. No one else knew what she had done. There was still time to turn back.

She picked up the phone and entered Glennie's number.

"Oh my God, Juliet. Where have you been?"

"I've been with him since Tuesday night."

There was an exhalation on the other end of the line.

"I've walked by your dark house every night and was worried sick. Are you okay?"

"Can you come over for a little while?"

"Of course."

Glennie abruptly hung up the phone.

Juliet did not move from her seat at the table. The day had become dull and dreary, and although a few lights would have made the room feel cheerier, she turned on none of them.

Glennie let herself in at the front door, kicked off her shoes and walked quickly back to the kitchen. The two women stared at each other.

"It's that bad, huh?" Glennie asked.

"Is it possible to be ecstatic and miserable at the same time?"

Glennie pulled a chair closer, took Juliet's hand and stroked it. She immediately noticed the black dirt under her fingernails, the greasy hair, and the soot on her face.

"Juliet, what's happening to you?"

"I really don't know where to begin. But, something is happening to me."

Glennie's eyes narrowed.

"Tell me what you mean."

"He's in me and through me. I ache to be with him. I've never, ever felt like this before, Glennie."

She held still, hoping Juliet would elaborate.

"It's like a wave I can't control. Like when you're caught in the ocean, and you want to fight your way back but you know it will tire you out. You just give in to the current and hope you'll wash up."

"Are you afraid to leave him?"

"Who? Skill or Charles?"

"Charles."

Juliet's eyes flashed.

"No. Why would you say that?"

"It's just that you seem mesmerized, like you're high. He's not hurting you, is he Juliet?"

Juliet closed her eyes and took a deep breath before opening them again.

"It's nothing like that, Glennie. He's kind and thoughtful. Even when we make love..."

Her voice trailed off. She looked down at the white and black tile design on the kitchen floor.

"Indescribable?"

"I'm transported. He studied Tantra in India. All I know is that we go on and on and on in ecstasy, spiritually and physically."

Glennie's eyes opened wider.

"One little touch makes my entire body quiver. I don't know how he does it. I'm almost out of my mind with desire."

She looked at Glennie.

"If you're safe and your bodies need each other, it must be Nature's will. Do you think he feels the same way?"

"I do. I don't have any gifts or cards or anything from him, but I know."

"So, you've been living with him in that abandoned cottage?" Glennie ventured.

"Yes. Can you believe I would spend so much time out in the cold?" There was irony in her weak smile.

"It does surprise me. What do you do all day? Besides have sex, that is."

"Glennie, he's sixty-three years old, so obviously, we're not having sex all the time. We keep the campsite maintained, gather wood, haul water, prepare food. Things like that. I'm actually learning a lot about surviving in the woods from him."

"But Juliet, what are you going to do when Skill gets home?"

"I don't want to think about it and waste any of our time on that. I know I have to face it eventually, though."

"When is he due back?"

"Not before Saturday. I really don't think he'll show up before then. You know how he is. He loves his schedules."

"I have to tell you something, Juliet."

"Okay. What?"

"Susan called me yesterday. She said she was worried about you. She wouldn't say why, but kept reminding me what a good friend you are."

Juliet brought her hand to her mouth, recalling the last time she saw Susan.

"Oh no. I had lunch with her and Lydia right after I slept with Charles. I was in such a rush. I just threw on my clothes. Do you think she knows?"

"No. I don't think she knows about Charles, but I do think she suspects you may be having an affair. She's very loyal to you, Juliet."

"But Lydia's not," Juliet said flatly.

Juliet woke in Charles' arms at the break of day on Saturday. He had already tended the fire but she would not yet leave the fur-piled bed. There would be much lovemaking and pillow talk first. She felt lithe and supple both inside and out; her muscles stretched in ways her body had never before been acquainted. A lingering soreness was the sweet reminder of the time she spent close to Charles. Every touch from this man introduced a bright, new perspective. With him, she felt like a river, flowing deep and slow, unobstructed. She had discovered the elusive balance between the pleasure of her own sensations and the simultaneous gift of rapture to another. It was the place where two become one.

The following days were intense with urgency. Juliet sucked up every drop of lust and love between them, as if the world's end was imminent. When alone, she considered what would become of them in a week's time, after her husband returned to Winston. She feared he would see the obvious: that she had been affected deeply by another man.

Days passed. Juliet collected and stored birch bark strips to use as fire starters when the woods were wet. She gathered rock tripe off boulders, washing it thoroughly to remove bitterness, then roasted it per Charles' instructions, until it was crisp and flavorful. This abundant lichen thickened soups and stews made with trapped birds and fish caught through a hole maintained in the ice. Adding olive oil Juliet brought from home provided nutritional fat that helped them stay warm.

At night, they sat side by side in their matching chairs, covered with furs. Charles pointed out constellations and retold ancient stories. They sang folk songs, laughing when they forgot the words. Illuminated by the light of an oil lamp hung from a tree limb, he read to her from "The Rubyiat." Juliet watched his eyes move back and forth across the page, the tip of his white beard changing shape as his mouth formed each word.

*Here with a Loaf of Bread beneath the Bough,*
*A Flask of Wine, a Book of Verse-and Thou*
*Beside me singing in the Wilderness-*
*And Wilderness is Paradise enow.*
And then,
*The Moving Finger writes; and having writ,*
*Moves on; nor all your Piety nor Wit*
*Shall lure it back to cancel half a Line,*
*Nor all your Tears wash out a Word of it.*
When Charles closed the leather-bound book, he explained its significance to him.

"My grandfather read these poems to me. First in the original Persian, then an English translation at the end of each quatrain. It was fascinating. The verses can be rearranged in a random manner to completely change the meaning. He told me this reflected life's transience."

Charles turned toward the glowing coals. "Life is transient, isn't it? I feel that acutely right now."

Balancing a coffee cup on its saucer, Susan walked over to the table in the Unitarian Universalist Fellowship Room where the petition lay ready to be signed. Judging from the number of people congregating around the table, she guessed the signature tally to have already reached one hundred.

Gil refused to sign. No surprise to her there. Susan picked up the pen and wrote her name. Just as she wrote the "w" at the end of Shaw, Lydia Randall sidled up next to her.

"I think he's a big fake," she said, out of the corner of her mouth.

"What do you mean?" Susan asked.

"Doesn't it seem odd that he just showed up out of nowhere and set up a tepee in the middle of a city?"

"I think it was a tent. But, yeah, it's strange. Maybe he needed to get away to heal some kind of trauma."

"That's ridiculous. If someone was really hurting, they'd probably hole up at home, not in some freezing shack. But who cares about that if he's an enormous hunk? Let's get someone to invite him to church so we can check him out!"

"Are you going to sign this?" Susan held up the pen.

"Oh, what the heck," Lydia answered, snatching the pen from Susan's hand.

The tradition of gathering informally after the service was always popular with inquisitive Unitarian Universalists, but today's coffee hour was particularly lively. The members were ignited with their favorite pastime: championing the underdog. On the other side of the room, underneath the dimpled glass of a large sun-filled window, Gil Shaw was standing among a circle of men. His hands were in his pockets and he was amusing himself rocking back and forth on his heels. The five other men listened intently to Evalynne Miller, Winston's Deputy District Attorney.

"It's a clear violation of city statutes," she explained.

"But it's not in keeping with the intent of the law," one of the men argued.

"There must be a precedent that can be used," said another.

"I'd be more than happy to listen to any contrary argument, but I have to tell you, gentlemen, this is a very flimsy case on his behalf."

The short man with the handlebar mustache spoke. "But 'Charlie' is harmless. He hasn't done anything wrong. And, he doesn't even have any decent representation!"

"I have an idea."

Everyone turned to Gil Shaw.

"Why don't we ask Skillman Grant to take the case pro-bono?"

"Is he here today?" Evalynne asked, scanning the room.

"No. He's out of town, but I'm sure he'll be back before the court date. I can give him a call tonight," Gil assured the group, satisfied he had solved their problem.

"When is the hearing?" someone asked.

"In two weeks. The day before the Royce Center thing," responded Evalynne.

"I'll draft a few members to stand at the courthouse in a of show support," said the mustachioed man.

Briefly home again, Juliet listened to her voice-mail.

"Message received, 9:37am."

"Hello Juliet. This is Claire Houghton. I hope I'm not calling you too early. It's so cold and dreary out today. I wonder if you'd like to come over for a cup of tea. I've just put some lemon poppy seed bread into the oven and I couldn't possibly finish it all by myself. Would 11:00 be a good time for you? I hope you can make it! Good bye, now."

Still in coat and boots, Juliet slouched over the counter, considering this invitation. It was highly unusual for Claire to call. Perhaps the elderly woman had a problem or needed something she felt uncomfortable asking for over the phone. She could probably manage to fit in a short visit with her frail neighbor. While she was home, Juliet only had to check her email and practice the cello. Next Saturday's debut was a little more than a week away.

She hung her coat on the back of a kitchen chair, then walked to the study and turned on the computer. It was a chore to check e-mail but she felt even more irresponsible not checking.

Naturally, there was a message from Skillman:

*Hello Jewels. I hope you're enjoying your time alone and getting lots done. It turns out we'll need a few more days on this end after all so I won't be home until next Friday morning instead of this weekend. I hope that doesn't mess anything up for you. I'll have to stop in at the office as soon as I get back to Boston but I'll be home before six. Peter Callandra wants us all to go out to dinner together that night. I said yes. Hope that's okay. Love, Skill*

*p.s. Are you planning to pick the kids up from the airport that afternoon? They can always take the shuttle if you're too busy.*

Juliet clicked "Reply."

*Hi Skill! All is well here. Sorry you have to stay another week but I understand. Okay about dinner with Glennie and Peter. I was planning to drive to Logan to pick up the kids but I'll be back in time.*

*Hugs, J*

Juliet turned off the computer, beaming. Another week with Charles! This was more than she hoped possible.

She walked to the living room and sat down at her cello. It was seriously out of tune. Juliet realized how long it had been since she last practiced. After the strings were in order, she tightened the hair on the bow, applied rosin, and warmed up with a few scales. The Swan sheet music rested on the ornate brass stand just as she had left it. It seemed a lifetime ago that she had dissolved in tears after playing. Leaning forward, she pushed the tiny red "record" button on the tape player set up next to her stool, then positioned herself regally, elbows poised like fulcrums, back straight, neck and legs relaxed.

Juliet soared through the piece, hardly noticing the effort it took. It was a pleasure, a delight. She had never before been able to simultaneously play and enjoy music; it had always been one or the other. Not quite trusting her own ears, she listened to the new recording. Flawless. By all accounts, Juliet was more than ready for her performance. Remembering her old music teacher's advice that a performer should always carry an extra set of strings with her, she made a mental note to visit the music store in the next few days to buy more.

It was almost eleven, so Juliet leaned the cello onto its stand and contemplated whether she should take anything from home to add to the campsite. This time, in response to Glennie's comment about her dark house, she would leave both the kitchen and the bathroom lights burning. She put on her coat and walked outside, definitively shutting the door behind her.

Arriving on the steps at the back of Claire Houghton's house a few minutes early, Juliet grabbed the shovel resting next to the door and chipped at some stubborn ice patches. Claire soon heard the chinking sound of metal against granite. She appeared, opening the door just a crack so as not to push the younger woman off the narrow surface.

"Good morning, Juliet! I'm happy you got my message. Can you stay for a few minutes, dear?"

"Morning, Claire. Yes, I'd love to stay and try some of that yummy poppy seed bread." Juliet smiled at the bright blue eyes set deep in the wrinkled face.

"Well then, come right in, dear!"

Leaning the shovel against the side of the house, she maneuvered around the partially opened door. The nostalgic aroma of recent baking transported Juliet to another era as she stepped across the threshold into a kitchen painted daffodil yellow with glossy white trim. Cheery gingham curtains accented the windows. It was hard to imagine that she and Claire Houghton had anything in common, besides being neighbors.

"May I take your coat?"

"Yes. Thank you."

Juliet removed her heavy coat and handed it to Claire, who quickly appeared overwhelmed by the heft of it. It smelled of stale campfire, but if Claire noticed, she gave no indication. Juliet remained standing until she returned to the kitchen.

"Please sit down and make yourself comfortable while I get our little treats ready," Claire said, busying herself at the counter.

Juliet studied the stooped shoulders and rounded back of the woman. The small gray bun at the top of her head bobbed up and down with an involuntarily palsy, the inevitable companion of aging.

"Can I help?" ventured Juliet.

"You sit tight right there and I'll be done in a minute. It's not often I have a guest to serve, you know."

Claire turned, carrying a tray, then set it down on the table. Arranged on it were a silver tea service, the poppy seed bread, and two neatly pressed ivory linen napkins, each embroidered with an olive-colored *H*.

When they both were seated, Claire ceremoniously offered cream and sugar for the tea and slices of the warm bread. The house was quiet except for the occasional creak of an old beam settling and the tick tock of the antique grandfather clock in the hallway. Just as Juliet ran out of small-talk topics, it became clear that Claire Houghton had a specific reason for inviting her to tea.

"Juliet?"

"Yes?"

"Do you remember my George?"

"Of course I do! He was so wonderful to all of us. I can't believe it's been five years since he's been gone."

She hoped the elderly woman was not troubled by her memories.

"He was a very good husband to me and a very good father to our children."

"I'm sure he was," Juliet said, sympathetically.

"I know I look like an old woman now, Juliet, but I was once young and considered very beautiful."

Juliet opened her mouth to speak but Claire held up a gnarled hand to stop her.

"George and I were married fifty-nine years before he died. For the most part, they were wonderful years, dear. But, we had our share of ups and downs, as most couples do."

Her blue eyes fixed on Juliet's.

"I was only nineteen years old on my wedding day. Back in that era, marriage was the beginning and end of your relationship with men."

Claire lifted the flower pattern porcelain tea cup to her lips. With her pinky finger extended, she took a dainty sip, then set the delicate cup gently down on its saucer, where it made a little "ping" sound.

"I'd always wondered what it would feel like to be with another man. It wasn't something girlfriends could discuss in my day, so I was left alone with my curiosity. Finally, when I was in my early fifties, I started to look at life differently."

Juliet held herself very still, unnerved by the old woman's candor. Claire slowly brought her napkin to her lips, dabbed at the right corner of her mouth, then just as slowly returned the cloth to her lap.

"I went through The Change of Life and my life really did change—I believe for the better—but it was a struggle for those who had to adjust to me. Especially for George. I suddenly decided I wanted more and I would not be limited by society's rules."

Claire took another leisurely sip of tea then set her cup down again.

"I took a lover, Juliet."

Juliet struggled to maintain her composure and conceal her shock.

Claire smiled demurely, acknowledging the other woman's discomfort.

"I know it must be hard to imagine when you look at me now. It was very hard for George when he found out. He didn't find out for quite some time. And, he only knew about one of the men."

Claire paused. "I hope I'm not embarrassing you, dear," she said, patting Juliet's dirty hand.

"No. Not at all. Please, go on with your story," Juliet said, mustering poise.

"There was something I needed to understand about myself. I think you may know what I'm talking about." She paused to clear her throat. "I needed to discover my own feelings. I actually felt as if it was a matter of life and death.

My life and my death. I wanted to avoid the hysteria I saw in my friends. I felt like they had compromised themselves in marriage. The women hoped their men would be faithful to them while they bore children and the men hoped the women would be faithful to them as they grew old and impotent. I never understood that. Why not agree to be monogamous in the childbearing years and then re-evaluate after the kids have grown and are gone? Wouldn't this work better for everyone?"

Juliet nodded dumbly in agreement.

"I only knew that *I* needed to reach out and grab what I wanted. I couldn't wait any longer for it to come to me. I loved George, but I was not living George's life. I was living mine."

Juliet readjusted herself in her chair.

"This caused many, many problems in my life, as I am sure you can imagine. But Juliet, I wouldn't deny myself any of those caresses if I could do it over again. I am sorry that I hurt George but as we grew older, he saw my experiences for what they were. It was just life. Those sexual experiences were separate from my love for him. A woman has a right to feel. It would be a shame to get to my age and look back knowing you had shortchanged yourself. You can't hold your desires prisoner forever."

She evaluated Juliet's face for comprehension. "Well. I'm certainly glad we were able to have this nice chat," she said crisply, rising from the table.

Stunned, Juliet almost missed Claire's signal that it was time for her to go.

Claire left the room and came back with the heavy coat.

"Be careful, Juliet," she said, as she helped the younger woman put her arms through her coat sleeves.

"I will," Juliet answered. She leaned over and kissed the soft wrinkled cheek. "Thank you," she whispered, then left the kitchen of Claire Houghton.

Aided by her unobstructed view of the path entrance, Claire had guessed what Juliet had been doing deep in the woods. The old woman was adept at picking up messages too subtle for someone less experienced at life. Wisely, she had shared her knowledge to help Juliet navigate through her rapidly transforming future. Although the conversation left her feeling somewhat infantile, she remained grateful.

When she reached the clearing, Charles was stacking kindling onto the woodpile, his back toward her. She stood there for a moment, contemplating the turn her life had taken. She had her own money and she didn't require marriage. There would be no more children. In her heart, in her mind, and yes, in her body, she knew she was undeniably in love. When Charles turned and waved, Juliet dropped her bag onto the snow and ran to him.

Early afternoon sun poured through the wavy glass of the cottage window and warmed Juliet's back where she sat knitting row after row of Charles' sweater. He had been deeply touched by her effort to create something unique and personal for him. As she progressed through the pattern, she occasionally held the evolving garment against Charles' frame for sizing; stretching it across his chest to gauge if it was broad enough, or holding a sleeve at his shoulder to see where it would fall at his wrist. Charles stood still as she fussed; the color of the yarn playing games with the green of his eyes; her nurturing and loving gestures bringing a smile to his lips. As for Juliet, she was grateful for the opportunity to offer some practical skill of her own to their daily life. It seemed the balance of useful expertise was nearly always tilted in Charles' favor.

At night, they read to each other. Later she would sit in the shadows, knitting in hand, determined to complete the sweater before the end of the week. One night, peering over the glint of his flute, Charles studied Juliet where she sat at the hearth, her face barely visible in the ember glow. Soft musical notes drifted in the air around them until he moved the flute a few inches from his lips.

"I still don't understand how you can knit in the dark. I need light for everything I do."

"But Charles, you were just playing the flute in the dark."

"Yes, but that's because I feel the flute when I play. You have to make many more motions than I do. I don't have to turn my flute when I play a new song like you turn your needles at the end of each row."

Charles' puzzlement was endearing. For the first time, he revealed a side of himself that seemed almost boyish. It reminded her of when she was little; when there was a clear delineation between all things boys and all things girls. The boys were forever making mistakes: misidentifying "ponytails" as "pigtails," or "skirts" as "dresses," as if these distinctions were too complex to fathom. The confusion delighted the girls.

"I feel my way through knitting, too, Charles. When I knit a stitch, my finger touches what I've done to make sure it's right. At the end of the row, I rub the work between my two fingers to see if anything feels abnormal."

"But what if you find you missed a mistake when you look at it the next day?" he persisted.

"Usually I can take one stitch out and undo it vertically. I follow it all of the way down to the row where I made the mistake."

"And if that doesn't work?"

"Then I have to rip out all of the rows."

Juliet put aside her knitting for the night. "It's like life. We hope we don't make mistakes but we always do. We can fix some the easy way but some take a lot more work. Everything can be fixed, if you know how."

"You said it right there. If you know how," Charles commented.

"Yes." She paused. "That's what I worry about. Will I be able to fix my mistakes? I don't think I know how."

"That's where faith enters. Living in the now, taking each moment and each day as it comes. It's exactly what we're doing, Juliet."

"I know. But there are so many things left for me to correct. Eventually, I'll have to face them. All at once."

Charles walked over to Juliet and pulled her up from her chair. "Let's forget the world for now."

As Juliet swept the cottage floor with the bough broom, she spotted a sketchbook wedged behind the shelves. Propping the broom against the wall, she picked up the pad and opened it to the first page. On it was a well-executed depiction of the old cottage. Turning the pages, she viewed charcoal illustrations of the entire campsite as well as renderings of some of the trees and favorite animals she and Charles often observed. She flipped eagerly through the book, pleased to discover another talent of the man she adored. Half-way through, she came upon a drawing of a sleeping woman. He had captured Juliet lying on their bed, partially covered by furs, one arm over her head, one breast exposed, a beatific expression on her face. She was warmed by this almost classical portrayal, reminiscent of a Greek sculpture, and wondered if Charles really saw her that way. It was his last entry.

He was outside preparing a fish for their lunch when Juliet approached him with the sketchbook.

"Charles, I was cleaning and came across this. I didn't mean to snoop but my curiosity got the better of me. I looked through the whole book. It's marvelous work. I had no idea you were an artist."

He took the pad from her and flipped through it. "I've been drawing most of my life. I've got no discipline though—just self-expression."

"I'd say you're quite good. I saw the drawing of me," she added, a little shyly.

"And? Did you like it?"

"Charles, it's gorgeous and terribly flattering. When did you do it?"

"Yesterday morning, after I finished rekindling the fire. Would you like me to sketch you again, now that you're awake?"

"I've never posed for an artist before. At least never while I was awake! But yes, thank you. I think I'd enjoy that very much."

"What artists do you like?" he asked.

"Let me think. Georgia O'Keefe. Mary Cassatt. Renoir. And also, this may sound strange, but I love Hieronymus Bosch, in a very prurient kind of way," she laughed.

"Why prurient?"

"I'm fascinated by the depravity of it and the way he depicts hell."

Juliet looked up at the sky and sighed. "I hope there is no hell because I might go there, the way I've been behaving."

"I see only goodness in you, Juliet."

Perhaps he saw only goodness in her because he only saw her in their little world, Juliet thought.

Charles picked up a cast iron pan. "Let's get this fish cooked and we'll turn our afternoon into a studio session."

Later that day, Charles doubled a pelt across one of the fireside rocks, then positioned a bundled Juliet over it. The afternoon light was perfect. Juliet squirmed a bit under the scrutiny of Charles' gaze.

He lowered the pad onto his thighs.

"Juliet?"

"Yes?"

"Does this make you uncomfortable?"

She took a deep breath. "I'm worried about what you'll see if you look at me so closely and for so long."

"Let me tell you what I'm looking at and hopefully that will relieve your anxiety."

Juliet furrowed her brow.

"It's true that I'm studying your features but I do that as a basis for the portrait. What I really try to see, Juliet, is the spirit within the features. It'll be something I find in your eyes or in a little wrinkle here or there. It can reveal a morsel about the life you've lived. Beyond that, I look for hints about your future from the energy you project. There may be a clue that tells me where you're going."

Juliet shook her head in amazement. "I'm floored. I had no idea portraiture was so complex."

Charles set down his tools, walked over to her and took her face into his hands.

"I've been studying you since we first met. Your face. Your body. I see a whole life story. It's subtle. It's intricate. It's unique. Everything you've ever done and everything you've ever felt is written all over you. That's what I'm trying to capture."

She soon appreciated the merits of being an artist's model. While Charles was intent on studying her, she was able to study him. His eyes focused on one area of her, then shifted to his sketchpad. With his head lowered, Juliet watched him as he became lost in concentration, pulling his lower lip under his front teeth, his big hand moving rapidly over the paper. Artist and subject were silent; other than the twitter of birds or the occasional squirrel chatter, the only noise was the irregular scratching of charcoal against paper. Charles raised his eyes again and again, roaming over her face and body for his next cue. Their silent exchange was erotically charged as they visually consumed one another, gorging on new information revealed that afternoon.

Over the following days, Charles filled his book with studies of Juliet. There were close-ups of her hands and feet; her shoulders; the back of her head; her nude body in repose. Charles posed her over furs on the cottage hearth, close to the blazing fire. He recorded every inch of her exterior but sought to capture the essence inside. It became another layer of love-making to them. Juliet relished the chance to revisit those moments again at another time by viewing the sheets of paper that Charles' hands transformed

.

The weather was suddenly warmer; one of the strange temperature swings characteristic of a New England winter. Melting snow mixed with defrosting dirt formed a soupy mud. Because it was such a fine day, Charles decided it would be a good opportunity to remove the branch of the old oak tree which threatened to fall on top of the woodpile and scatter the logs he had neatly stacked. Even with Juliet's help, this pruning was a huge job. Both of them were soon drenched with sweat and splattered with mud.

At about 10am, as they sat quietly by the fire pit, taking a much needed break from their labor, they heard voices in the woods. Juliet's eyes flew open. She looked at Charles with mute alarm, then dashed inside the cottage for cover, out of sight and hearing. Charles didn't stir. He waited patiently in his chair for the arrival of the strangers.

In a few moments, two men and a woman appeared in the clearing. Charles slowly raised his massive frame to greet them.

"Hello," he said cordially.

"Good morning," the short stout man with the red hair and handlebar mustache responded. The two others smiled and nodded timidly behind him. It seemed to Charles that their arrival had the mark of rehearsed choreography. He remained silent, politely waiting for the group to reveal their intention.

"We're here representing the Unitarian Universalist Fellowship of Winston," their leader began in a shaky voice. "We'd like to welcome you to our community and we'd like to invite you to one of our services."

Apparently, they didn't feel it was necessary to burden this feeble-minded hermit with cumbersome details such as their names. The three huddled close together, looking up at the much taller Charles. He held every advantage in this interaction and might have played longer with this group, had Juliet not been nervously waiting in the rehabilitated cottage.

"This is very kind of you," he replied, and then went silent again, unwilling to offer any information about his future plans.

The contingent exchanged nervous glances, interspersed with silent gestures encouraging their leader to continue. He finally did.

"We're aware that our town has cited you for various violations. We want you to know that we not only applaud your choice to live in an alternative manner but we'd also like to offer legal and emotional support to you at your upcoming hearing."

Charles' eyes crinkled at the corners. "I'm grateful to you and your members. Thank you very much indeed."

The trio would have liked to learn more about the reasons this hermit decided to set up a home in the winter woods but it was clear to them that Charles would not be forthcoming with any information. As Unitarian Universalists, they respected his right to follow, without hindrance, his own independent search for truth and meaning.

"Thank you very much for your time," the stout man said. Deflated at the prospect of returning to town with so little information, he felt some satisfaction that he had at least delivered the committee's message.

With the end of their meeting acknowledged, the threesome tried surreptitiously to catch a glimpse of the campsite behind Charles. This proved difficult for them because Charles' imposing stature and ability to command all eyes to his, prevented it. Ultimately, they turned away and walked silently back into the woods; the heat of his gaze causing them to hurry down the path. When they got to the bridge on Concord Street, the would-be ambassadors formed a huddle.

"That was one impressive giant of a man," said the woman.

"Do you think we offended him, just showing up like that?"

"Perhaps." Breathing heavily after the hike, their leader launched his assessment. "I don't think we've done any harm that can't be easily rectified when he comes to one of our services. It's important for someone like him, so obviously lacking social structure, to feel that not everyone in our town is against him, and to feel that the constraints of convention will not be a factor in our unconditional acceptance and support of him. It's certainly a good thing that Skillman Grant has agreed to represent him at next week's hearing."

Charles returned to the fire pit and sat down in his chair, waiting for Juliet to reappear. This was the first time any foreigner had entered their blissful woods. Juliet's reaction the moment she realized a violation of their sanctity was imminent, betrayed her fear. It was a painful reminder of reality and the outside world they tried to ignore.

"Charles," Juliet said softly, joining him by the fire. Her eyes darted around the woods. She had heard and seen nothing, hidden in the cottage.

"Yes?"

"Do you think they'll come back?"

"No. I think they did what they wanted to do, Juliet," he said, looking up at her. "You're afraid, aren't you?"

Juliet sank her forehead into her dirty hands.

"Why can't everyone just leave us alone?"

He sighed and stood up next to her.

"Juliet, the world is out there."

"I know! I just don't want it to come in here. This is our world!" she said, looking up at him, tears in her eyes.

Charles waited.

"What did they say?" she asked.

"They want me go to church."

Charles decided not to tell Juliet about the citation, given the fragile notion she had about their privacy. He considered telling her eventually, when she was stronger.

Although her appearance was less than fastidious after so many days at the cottage, Juliet left Charles at the edge of the clearing late Wednesday morning and set out to purchase additional cello strings, and also check the status of her house. She moved through the woods toward the Concord Street bridge, deep in thought about this new intimate relationship.

It was unbalanced. Charles indulged her desire to reveal almost nothing about herself but answered every question Juliet asked of him. She asked few though, not wanting to feel obliged to reciprocate with answers of her own. He did not pry or persist if she left out details that should have been a natural part of their mutual understanding.

There was greed in wanting two worlds for herself: the stable foundation she had with Skillman and their children, in addition to the passionate, exclusively adult romance she had with Charles. It was a dangerous calculation. Women had been known to share one man with several females, but was there a man alive who would willingly share his woman with even one other man?

She arrived at Nuttings Music. The store windows were plastered with an assortment of fliers announcing instruments for sale and various community events. Most prominent was a poster board covered with bold green ink.

At the top was an image of the Celtic "Green Man." Her eyes attacked the text.

*LET CHARLIE BE!*

*A noble heritage of outstanding individuals have chosen to live in Nature. Thoreau himself lived for two years on Walden Pond, only a few miles from Winston. Now, here in Winston itself, we have our very own Thoreau—"Charlie"— who lives peacefully in the woods of our town. Regulations prohibit living on land without appropriate deeds, permits and inspections, but if an individual is capable of living a safe life without these restrictions, and is no danger to others, is the spirit of the law violated?*

*We believe that each person has an inherent worth and dignity and that every person should be free to search for personal truth and meaning in the manner they envision. With that in mind, we invite you to sign the petition below to support a suspension of the regulations and sanctions against this peaceful individual.*

*The Unitarian Universalist Fellowship of Winston*

Juliet's reaction to the caricature of Charles as a "Green Man" was swift; although these people knew absolutely nothing about him they were effectively building a mythology and spreading word of his plight throughout the community. She yanked open the store door, purchased her strings, and left.

Skillman's return was imminent. With a good plan, she hoped to move through the important weekend without her secret being revealed. All three kids, including Deirdre, would arrive in Winston on Friday and her family would be reunited. The prospect sent simultaneous waves of joy and sadness through Juliet's heart. Charles would be alone at the cottage, cognizant that Juliet had chosen her family over him; easily concluding she was ashamed of him and their romance.

If having an affair was not complicated enough, Juliet knew people would not see Charles the way she saw him. To them, he would be "Charlie" the hermit, a wild looking giant of a man with dirty fingernails and piercing green eyes. Winston was her town and she knew how quickly its residents could spring to vicious judgment. They would not evaluate Charles with kindness once they learned he had been romancing one of their established married residents.

Juliet vowed never to let details of her affair be known, even though she had no idea how she would prevent it. If Claire Houghton had dissolved Juliet's cover simply by speculating that she was a woman with an itch, how many others would suspect there was something different about Juliet and arrive at a similar conclusion?

At the rear of Nine Chestnut Street, Juliet draped her coat over the porch railing, leaving the garment's odor outside. Inside, she set about perusing the house for evidence that might reveal her unusual activity.

In the bedroom, she pressed to her face articles of clothing worn at the campsite, investigating them for the acrid smell of stale smoke. Gathering all the offending pieces, she carted them to the basement and loaded them into the washer. She scoured the bathroom, changed the master bedroom sheets, and dusted and vacuumed the main rooms to support the appearance of having kept up with home life in Skillman's absence. She selected what she would need in the near future: underwear, a complete outfit, a coat, and a pair of dressy shoes. As an extra precaution, she double-bagged these fresh clothes against any danger of penetrating camp odors, then carried the bundle downstairs.

Juliet cleaned everything but her own body. In that respect, she would stay true to Charles.

There was no time to indulge in sentiment while preparing the former rooms of her children. She set about making their beds and laying out fresh towels.

In the kitchen, she scanned the refrigerator shelves for any perishable food overlooked earlier in the week. Tossing offenders into the trash, she sprayed the interior with vinegar-water and wiped down the cold, empty shelves.

Fishing cello strings out of her pants pocket, she took the little pouch to the living room and stowed it in the cello case as emergency insurance for Saturday's event. If she practiced her music alone one last time early Friday afternoon, then performed a rehearsal in front of her family sometime early on Saturday, she was confident her performance would be more than satisfactory. With the myriad of details and quandaries consuming her now, anxiety about her cello debut had faded from her list of priorities.

Juliet plopped down in a chair at the kitchen table to contemplate her immediate future. Today was Wednesday. Thursday night would be her last night alone with Charles until her family left on Sunday. After that, who knew when, or even if, she could manage to slip out at night while Skillman slept.

Forcing herself to focus on a multitude of tasks would keep her one step ahead of personal disaster. It was her best hope. A supreme effort would be needed to restore her previous appearance. As a start, she thumbed through the phone book for a new beauty salon located steps away from a "T" stop, then made a Friday morning appointment, using an assumed name.

Charles' recollection of an immaculately groomed version of Juliet was fading. She preferred he keep the austere image, wanting him to see her in the most unmitigated way. Once they had become intimate, she had used no female sleight of hands to enhance her beauty; she never doubted that he found her most attractive when she was genuine and natural in both affect and physical presentation.

There were household details to tend to as well. Left still was planning a trip to the supermarket. With a pencil and pad in hand, she listed each item she needed in the order it appeared in the store, facilitating a speedy trip at the end of the week. When the alarm announced the end of the dryer cycle, she rushed downstairs to fold the clothes, completing the final domestic task.

One last time, Juliet surveyed the appearance of the main floor, gathered together the bags at the doorway, then stepped back outside into the cold. Draped over the railing for hours, her coat was nearly frozen, but Juliet hardly noticed as she pushed her arms through the sleeves and continued her mission. First, garbage bags were dropped into trash cans. Next, Juliet opened the car door and positioned the grocery list on the center of the dashboard where she could locate it easily on Friday morning. Finally, she scooped up her bag of clean clothes and hurried back down the alley to the one she loved most.

Charles and Juliet abandoned all non-essential chores, spending what little time they had left in each other's arms. Their sexual journey was one Juliet could never have imagined possible a few short weeks ago. Charles had taught Juliet how to master her carnal sensations. Quite often for her there was no beginning, no middle, no end; only a continuum of awareness and receptivity. They refrained from judgment; no position, feeling, or movement was unacceptable. There was no "doing," only "being." Leaving all of their emotional and physical memories in the past left only the present. The separate energies of Charles and Juliet had coalesced.

Friday's dawn was red. Naked and silent, they held each other close. Juliet strained to release herself from her own flesh, pressing fully onto Charles, willing herself to become a part of him. It could not be done, of course. As she wept, he kissed away each tear. Later, at the edge of the clearing, Juliet stumbled down the familiar path toward Concord Street, choking back sobs.

A small number of people waited at the train station platform. Few commuters would head outbound, away from the city at this hour. Juliet easily found an empty seat on the train and settled the thick garbage bag of clothes on her lap. When the train pulled away, the motion rocked her gently, as it had so often in the past. An elderly woman shot a once-over glance in her direction, shook her head, then turned away. The two men sitting across from her exchanged glances, then leered at her. Finally, the young woman Juliet hoped was an ally, covered her mouth and nose, then stood and moved to a new location.

When squeaky brakes announced her destination, she clutched her garbage bag, grateful to escape the train. The brick facade of the Dyson Health Center was familiar and the buff desk clerk had not changed, but everything seemed different for Juliet now.

A few twists of the combination opened the locker door. She stood there dazed for a moment, overwhelmed by the myriad of products stacked neatly on the shelf: blonde highlight activating shampoo and deep penetrating hair conditioner; a sealed pack of pink, double-blade razors; collagen-fortified moisture lotion.

Finally, Juliet pulled her shirt over her head and slipped off her pants.

A petite woman passed by, quickly averting her eyes. Juliet pressed the soiled garment against her chest, grabbed her towel and took cover in a dressing room, sweeping the curtain across the rod with a flourish. She reminded herself of the conventional notions of privacy, as old patterns of shame threatened to return. Had she forgotten the way the rest of the world would respond? To stop the flow of fresh tears, she bit her lip, then, modestly covered by a towel, she sought a vacant shower stall.

Surrounded by steam, hot water pelting her from above, Juliet began the arduous task of restoring her body to its former appearance. Twice, she vigorously shampooed and rinsed her hair. Tracks from the fresh razor on her underarms and legs felt distressingly raw. A stiff nail brush rubbed back and forth across her fingernails and toenails removed most of the dirt and soot lodged underneath.

With the towel wrapped once again around her torso, she scrutinized her appearance at the sink. At close range, she noted the sticky yellow plaque on her teeth, the unkempt eyebrows, the stray hairs on her chin, and the clogged pores on her nose. After resting an assortment of department store makeup on the shelf, she began to counter her offenses: a concealer to mask dark circles; a pasty eye-lid primer to reduce creasing; soft brown shadow for emphasis; bone-colored shadow to highlight the brow area; gray eyeliner for definition; brow powder to fill in the sparse areas; black-brown waterproof mascara to give the illusion of lash fullness and length. A little blush, and the palette would be nearly perfect. For the final touch, she twisted a rose colored pillar out of the lipstick tube and ran it over her lips, filling the bow shape of her sad mouth. What once seemed a tasteful accentuation of her beauty, now seemed false and garish. The mask was complete.

Inside the curtained dressing room, there was no need to view her naked body in the mirror. She saw it now in her mind's eye. As she fastened the back of a stiff bra, the memory of Charles' enormous hands on her breasts made her catch her breath.

The pink angora sweater and lined wool pants she had previously selected felt moderately comfortable. Her feet were another story. Only a few hours ago, she had wiggled dirty toes inside old soft boots; a luxury impossible to replicate in stiff leather dress shoes.

Juliet jammed the double-wrapped acrid smelling clothes into her locker, clanged it shut, then walked briskly out of the building to the tap-tap tune of dainty soles.

Under a brilliant sun, Charles welcomed this first real thaw that cracked the rigid back of winter. Soon days would grow longer, animals would reemerge, buds would burst from supple tree branches. He knew that maple tree sap was already running, but regretted there would be no opportunity to tap these woods.

Charles took a deep breath and pulled his posture ramrod, reveling in the feeling of immense stature. From the small eel-skin case where his passport and essential documents of civilization were stored, he removed the summons and tucked it into his back pocket. The hearing was scheduled for one o'clock, leaving several hours to clean the cottage and surrounding campsite. The judge would most certainly rule in favor of the Town of Winston and he would then be forced to vacate the cottage and seek accommodation elsewhere.

Whistling, he straightened the kitchen area, neatly stacking all of the cooking tools in one place, then scattered the bulk of remaining food outside for animals to eat. Almost immediately, squirrels and birds found the leftover grains and nuts at the base of the large oak tree. He tossed the furs over there as well; they would be pecked and pulled at for nest matter until tattered. The remaining pelts would decompose from spring rain.

Charles' philosophy had always been to live in the moment. Agonizing about circumstances over which he had no control seemed counterproductive. In fact, he welcomed the prospect of interesting changes that might appear over the next few days.

He unfolded the soft green sweater and pulled it over his head. It was perfect for the day's weather and he was glad to have something clean to wear to town. He reviewed the summons once more, carefully refolded it into a neat square and returned it to his pocket, then set out along the muddy path to Concord Street. Even at a leisurely pace, his long stride brought him to the courthouse earlier than necessary, providing an opportunity to establish the lay of the land and visit a conventional bathroom. He was curious to view the mark a woods lifestyle had left on him.

At the urinals, a nondescript man's eyes followed the hermit's feet as he walked toward the mirror. A grin spread across Charles' face when he saw his reflection: long hair matted beyond redemption and wrinkles that appeared almost tattooed on his face. Twisting the cold water faucet handle, he cupped his hands and took a hearty drink, then brushed away the beads of water nestled on his full beard.

At the sink, the other man washed his hands, pulled a few pieces of gray paper from the wall dispenser, then spoke.

"You must be 'Charlie.'"

"I guess I can answer to that."

The man smiled affably, extending a dried hand.

"I'm Attorney Skillman Grant. I'm going to represent you at your hearing today." He spoke slowly and deliberately.

They shook. Skillman's hand was swallowed by Charles' grasp.

Charles looked down at the shorter man. "I imagine I don't have much of a case."

"Well, things are stacked against you but you've got considerable support in the community. Let's take a few minutes and discuss the details in the conference room. Would you like a cup of coffee?"

Charles shook his head.

Skillman switched to lawyer mode, gratefully falling back on his training in this awkward situation where he now found himself. He had expected a persona non grata. Discovering an intelligent man in no apparent distress despite exposure to months of winter weather was unsettling. The penetrating green eyes and overall physicality were difficult to dismiss. He exuded uncommon power and charisma; truly a "man's man" in every respect. Reflexively, Skillman found himself uncomfortably aware of his masculine shortcomings.

He held the bathroom door open for "Charlie." As they walked down the hall toward the conference room, the noise from a crowd outside drew their attention. Thirty people holding signs chanted, "Let Charlie Be! Let Charlie Be!" Supportive honks from passing cars stoked their enthusiasm to a fever pitch.

Skillman looked up at Charles. "There's your fan club, but I'm not sure they'll make a difference."

Charles raised his eyebrows then followed him into the small conference room. Skillman turned to shut the door behind them. At the gleaming table where they sat, Charles crossed his long legs, leaned back in his chair and waited for the attorney's next move.

"Excuse me for just one moment, please." Skillman stood to prop open the door, pausing for a gulp of hallway air before returning.

At the table, he outlined Charles' offense.

"Town of Winston regulations specifically prohibit the temporary or permanent residence of anyone in a dwelling not inspected and approved by the code enforcement officer. Do you understand that your living arrangement would be categorized as a condemned structure?" Skillman directed the question to Charles while opening a slender manila case folder.

"I suppose by some standards that could be considered true," Charles replied, never taking his eyes off the attorney.

Skillman adjusted the cuffs of his shirt, brought his hands to the table again and folded them.

"It'd be easier for me if I had a sense you wanted to win this case," he said to Charles.

"Look, I've stayed at the cottage many times, although not in the past forty years. It's far away from everything and everyone, so I'm puzzled why it's of any concern to the town. I'm really not trying to be difficult, Stewart," Charles replied, in a friendlier tone.

"It's Skillman."

"Sorry. Skillman."

"Okay. Let's see what we have here." Skillman rifled through the papers in the folder.

Charles pulled the legal pad and pen toward him. "Here's what I think you should use as my argument."

Charles deftly diagrammed his strategy while a tight lipped Skillman summoned patience. After digesting the proposal, Skillman chuckled appreciatively. "You've been to law school, haven't you?

"I didn't finish but I stayed long enough."

"Suppose I use your defense and the judge doesn't go for it?" Skillman asked.

"I'll be no worse off. You know as well as I do that a case like this will almost always go down. The judge won't want to set precedent. I'm willing to live with the consequences." He leaned back in his chair again, lacing the fingers of his hands together behind his head.

"All right, then. Let's do it." Skillman closed the folder, pushed his chair back, and stood.

Charles remained seated. "Skillman?" he said, looking up at him.

"Yes?"

"I appreciate your effort. I know you're doing this pro-bono. It takes a good man to defend a cause that's important to others."

Skillman smiled. He knew Charles had deliberately remained seated out of deference to him.

When he rose, towering over him again, they exchanged a warm handshake.

Sunshine-colored highlights processed inside foil squares woven into the hair on Juliet's scalp. Viewed from behind, she was a comical sight. On the opposite side of the table, her manicurist gathered a different impression. The technician examined the limp hands of her morose customer, turning and twisting both in critical assessment.

"Do you spend a lot of time outdoors?" the woman asked.

"No."

"Your hands are extremely dry. I'm going to have to cut the nails very short since they're in such poor condition," she apologized.

"Go ahead."

Juliet glanced over at the clock.

"We could do a paraffin dip to seal some moisture into your skin," the woman offered. "There's also a special today on our lavender soak."

"I don't have time."

Two and a half hours later, Juliet left the salon and walked the short distance to the "T" stop where a young woman stood on the platform holding the hands of her two small children. She smiled at Juliet.

"Your hair looks so pretty. Would you mind telling me where you get it done?"

"It's a place down the street on the left. I'm sorry, but I don't remember the name," Juliet answered. She struggled to find even those words.

"Thanks, anyway. Not that I have time to get my hair done with these guys," she said, using her head to point toward the children whose little hands held tight in her own.

Juliet softened. "Don't worry. It'll get easier in some ways."

On the train, she moved far down the aisle in order to sit alone during the short trip to Winston.

At the entrance to the path on her way home, she mustered resolve to pass by it. In her imagination, she conjured up the savory aroma of a fish, carrot, and turnip sauté she envisioned Charles cooking for lunch. He'd take the heavy pan to the edge of the reservoir and rinse it at the section where the ice always melted. Perhaps that friendly little squirrel would be perched on a long branch of the oak tree, anticipating the treat Charles would leave. A little later, he would add a log to the fire and pull his chair close so he could read a few pages from his book. He'd fall into the luxury of a brief afternoon nap. Bruised by a memory of previously doing all these things with Charles, Juliet ached with the uncertainty about ever doing them again.

She turned down the alley. There was Claire, wearing red boots, scraping some icy slush off the surface of her porch. They waved to one another. The perceptive old woman would have noted Juliet's groomed transformation and probably guessed what would happen next in her life.

Juliet envied her ability to see the future.

In her own driveway, she unlocked and opened the door of the sleek Mercedes. It had been weeks since she had driven anywhere, but sliding now onto the leather seat and turning the ignition key, it felt like just yesterday. The seats warmed quickly and hot air soon blasted throughout the interior. Juliet snatched the grocery list left on the dashboard, folded it in half and tucked it into her purse. Grasping the steering wheel, she inhaled and exhaled deeply, searching for equilibrium. She had decided to pay the price of today's hectic schedule in exchange for the previous uninterrupted day with Charles. Shifting the car into reverse, she backed out of the driveway, leaving a white puff of exhaust in her wake.

In contrast to the frugality of the last few weeks, the experience of an American supermarket was surreal. The insipid music, the colorful packaging, the antiseptically clean floors, and the endless displays of food set Juliet's nerves on edge. A myriad of convenient ready-to-eat containers beckoned at every turn. Juliet consulted her list, then collected and placed each item onto the bottom of the metal cart.

She blended well with other shoppers. No one could have guessed the morning's dramatic transformation. Gone were the forest debris and acrid smell of campfire; sap no longer glued earth to her fingertips; remnants of hedonistic activity were erased. Her exterior was neutralized, compatible with conventional taste. After the clerk finished packing her canvas bags, Juliet pushed the heavy cart to her car and loaded the groceries into the trunk.

At home in her kitchen, she reviewed the plan for the remainder of the day while putting everything neatly away. Naturally, she would be happy to see the children that afternoon; not really children anymore, of course, but young adults. It wasn't often they were together as a family and she was touched that each of them had made an effort to come home to support her. They would have no idea how the nature of her needs had changed. As preoccupation with Charles escalated, and distress about her deteriorating marriage grew, anxiety about performing in front of others had evaporated.

It was almost three o'clock. Juliet willed herself to be strong for the sake of her children.

At Logan Airport, she noted her car's location in Central Parking, then navigated the maze to the baggage claim area where they agreed to meet. Juliet was early. She bought a cup of Dunkin' Donuts tea and found a seat in an empty row of chairs.

There had been a time in her life when she imagined herself independent and brave, visiting international airports, confidently enjoying new people and new places. It was a dream deferred. First there was marriage; then children; then finances and college tuition. Travel became a family matter where she measured her ability to efficiently pack and tend to the needs of others.

A parade of travelers marched in front of her now. Bored and haggard businesspeople, exhausted by delays and dehydrating cabins, trailed carry-on luggage behind them. Struggling parents juggled very young children and their formidable paraphernalia.

At last, there was the sound of familiar laughter. On the escalator was Jonus, looking relaxed and happy in his baggy pants, a knapsack slung over his strong shoulder. Behind him were two beautiful women, Deirdre and Althea, both looking vibrant, enjoying one another as they teased their brother a few steps below them.

Juliet took advantage of this moment to bask in the magnificence of her creations. Surely, her children were her heaven. She would live on forever through these good people, and with luck, countless generations would follow. Juliet stood and called out to them. They turned toward her with smiles of love, and her joy knew no bounds.

They drove away from the airport with Althea at the wheel. They had seen each other just recently at Christmas, but circumstances change rapidly in the lives of young adults. Juliet challenged herself to stay current about details surrounding different jobs, friends and activities.

Sometimes, her best strategy was listening.

"All of the women I meet are too serious," Jonus complained.

"That's because guys are spending all their time on computer games and don't know how to have intelligent conversations," Deirdre countered.

"When, or if, I ever get married, I'm marrying someone who won't nag me about how I spend my time."

"Maybe your wife will just have to find something better to do if you don't pay enough attention to her," Deirdre said.

They turned to Juliet, anticipating her usual mediation. Their mother simply shrugged her shoulders. Juliet didn't feel in a position to tell her kids what she thought was right and wrong anymore. As her own life evolved, she would have to let go of some of the details of theirs. Somehow, she must find her way back to being herself first, and a mother, second.

Althea pulled into the driveway and parked beside Skillman's Lexus. The "kids" tumbled out, noisily collected their carry-on luggage from the rear of the car, then bounded up the smooth granite steps to the house. Their father saw them drive up and heard the commotion. He was pulling open the door as they reached it.

There were hugs, one by one, as Skillman greeted and inspected his son and two daughters. Juliet followed the family inside and quietly shut the door behind her. She hung back until Skillman finished his boisterous reunion with the Grant trio. He caught her eye as he listened to one final story before the three young adults left their parents to settle into their old rooms.

With just the two of them in the kitchen, Skillman greeted her.

"Hello, Jewels."

He reached out to hug his wife. Over his shoulder, Juliet fought for composure, weakening with the pain of betrayal and despair about her situation. Skillman sensed her reserve but had grown accustomed to its recurring pattern and the distance between them. He released her and took a step back.

"You look beautiful. Is that a new sweater?" He knew many husbands ignored small things their wives did to look attractive and appealing.

"Thanks. No. I've had this for a while."

"It sounds like the kids already made plans for tonight, just like we thought they would. We should probably get ready for dinner with Peter and Glennie. The Martini Grill reservation is for 6:30."

"Sounds great. I've wanted to try that new place."

"I said we'd drop over to their house for a drink first, then drive to the restaurant together."

"I'd better get going then," Juliet said, turning toward the back stairs.

"I'll bring you up a glass of wine."

The second level was noisy as the kids moved back and forth between each room. Everyone except Juliet felt transported back in time as they settled into their old environment. The kids were fresh and full of life, but Juliet felt suddenly aged, exhausted by the weight of duplicity.

Jonus' ride arrived first; Althea and Deirdre raced off in Juliet's car soon after. The change of atmosphere was as swift as the entrance and exit of a tropical rainstorm.

A click from heels on wood announced Juliet as she walked down the back stairs, empty wine glass in hand. She wore a short black velvet skirt, black stockings and an electric blue blouse with the top few buttons left unfastened.

Skillman called from the hallway closet, "Which coat do you want to wear?"

"My black leather one, please."

He returned to the kitchen with Juliet's coat and held it so she could slip her arms through the sleeves.

"Thanks, Skill."

"Anytime, anything, anyhow for you, Jewels."

A resplendent Glennie opened the door, eyes wide once Skillman passed. Juliet shook her head quickly from side to side, indicating that the subject they were dying to discuss would be off limits, at least for now. Glennie squeezed her hand while the four of them walked into the living room.

"So, how was that vacation, Skill?" Peter asked.

"I don't think I'd call three weeks in Omaha a vacation," he shot back, rolling his eyes.

The two women got busy chatting and filling their wine glasses.

"I hear those Midwest nights can get pretty cold." Peter winked conspiratorially at Skillman.

"How's business this month, Peter?" Skillman quickly changed the subject.

The men fell into predictable topics of mutual interest, while Glennie seized the opportunity to pull Juliet into the next room.

"What has been going on with you?" she whispered. "Do you realize there's a rumor you're having a nervous breakdown?" Glennie kept an eye on the men.

"Oh, god! Are you serious?"

Glennie tilted her head to one side and sighed.

"I wonder if Skill has heard anything," Juliet worried.

"I don't think so. Peter would have mentioned it to me. They keep in touch. At least Skill uses a cell phone."

"Sorry." Juliet shrugged.

"Well, I must say, you've never looked better. Your skin is glowing and you're moving like a cheetah. It would help if you smiled once in a while, though," Glennie said, touching Juliet's elbow gently.

"Someday, I'll tell you everything, Glennie. Right now, I just have to get through this weekend. All three of the kids are home, you know."

"Maybe that will keep you and Skillman from getting too intense."

"I really hope so." Juliet's voice trailed off.

"It's time to go, ladies!" Peter's voice boomed through the room.

The Martini Grill was about twenty minutes away, but because Peter had some classical guitar music he insisted they listen to, conversation was kept to a minimum. When they arrived at the restaurant, they were seated immediately at an excellent table with a surrounding view of the Boston skyline. It was a romantic setting and the kitchen aromas forecast delicious options. The men ordered scotch, Glennie and Juliet ordered specialty martinis, and they soon fell into affable and effervescent conversation. Juliet was surprised to find herself enjoying the evening in spite of its complications. When Skillman offered a few jokes with uncharacteristic good timing, an astonished Juliet looked over at her husband with fresh eyes.

After the main course, the women, tipsy from the effects of martinis and dinner wine, excused themselves to visit the restroom together. As soon as the door closed behind them, Glennie bent down and looked under the stalls to ensure they were alone.

"You seem to be doing okay," she said.

"I'm just trying to be in the moment. No sense in wasting my life." Juliet applied a fresh coat of lipstick at the mirror.

"You really do look ravishing. There definitely is something different about you."

"Are you making a pass at me?" Juliet asked with a straight face.

This sent both women into a fit of giggles.

Glennie continued. "No, seriously, you're oozing."

"Maybe it's from all the incredible sex I've been having." Juliet raised her eyebrows suggestively.

Glennie addressed Juliet's mirror reflection. "If you're not careful, you might get some tonight. Have you noticed how Skill has suddenly turned into the life of the party?"

"He does seem rather full of himself."

"Raaather!" Glennie feigned an affected accent and held the door open for Juliet.

When the women returned to the table, they found desserts to share between them, along with a generous selection of complimentary cordials, courtesy of the management.

It had been a delightful evening. With the restaurant set to close, Skillman volunteered to go out into the cold night and warm up the car, while an equally chivalrous Peter stayed behind to help the women get their coats. Much of the restaurant staff had already left because of the late hour. As the three of them headed to the attendant-free coat room, Glennie excused herself to visit the ladies room before the ride home. Juliet took Peter's arm like an old friend, and they continued walking together down the hallway.

The dimly lit coat room was empty of patrons when they stepped inside to retrieve their coats. With one swift movement, Peter quickly shut the door and roughly pushed Juliet against the wall. Suddenly, his mouth was on hers and his hands were cupping her from behind, forcefully pulling her toward him. Juliet jerked out of his grasp.

"What are you doing?" she hissed with alarm.

"As if you don't know." Peter was derisive. "You've been sending me signals all night like a bitch in heat." He was trying again to pin her to the wall, but Juliet struggled, empty coat hangers clinking around her head. Peter's breath was hot with the heavy smells of dinner.

"Peter, let go of me!" Juliet disengaged herself, grabbed her coat and opened the door. She heard Peter snicker behind her.

It was impossible to face Glennie after this incident, so she quickly left the restaurant to join Skillman in their car. For once, she appreciated the predictable steadiness of his personality. On the ride home, the others kept up a constant chatter, with Juliet joining in only occasionally. Glennie assumed her friend was preoccupied with thoughts of Charles, so when they arrived at the Callandra home, she leaned over the front seat and patted Juliet's shoulder encouragingly, then gave her a quick kiss on the cheek. After saying good bye to Skillman, Peter leaned over to Juliet as well, positioning himself for the appearance of a platonic peck on her cheek. With Skillman busy adjusting the car heater, Peter pressed his face against the ear of the other man's wife and introduced the tip of his tongue."

"You're awfully quiet," Skillman ventured as they pulled away from the Callandras'.

"I guess all that food and drink caught up with me."

"It was fun though, wasn't it?"

Juliet looked over at him. "I actually had a great time, Skill."

"Me, too, Jewels."

Skillman reached out in the dark car to find his wife's hand and held it in his lap until they pulled into their driveway.

The house was dark. Althea, Deirdre and Jonus would not return home until the early morning hours. Saturday and Sunday would give them lots of time together as a family until it was time for them to move on again.

In the kitchen, Skillman flipped on the light switch, then took their coats to hang in the hall closest. While he was gone, Juliet considered Peter's brazen conduct in the restaurant coat room and later in the car. Her stomach fluttered. Had Glennie told Peter about Charles? Having kept so many confidences over the years, Juliet trusted her without reservation. Ruling that out, it was difficult to explain Peter's assertion that she was sending signals, and alarming to think her demeanor could have changed so significantly without her making an effort. It was true that she felt highly erotic. Charles awakened that dormant part of her, and with it, a myriad of unforeseen complications. Concluding that Peter must have been more intoxicated than he appeared, she pushed his behavior out of her mind, confident he would apologize at the first opportunity.

There was enough to occupy her mind right now without adding anything else to the mix.

Skillman returned to the kitchen.

"How about a nightcap?" He took two tiny glasses from the back of the top shelf and set them on the counter. "Remember these?"

"Yes, I do. I bought them at the thrift store for a quarter each."

"Those were the days, huh?" Skillman smiled as he filled the cordial glasses with liquor.

"Let's sit on the living room couch. We never do that anymore."

He threw a backward glance at Juliet while carrying the brimming glasses of liquor into the next room. "I set up some logs in the fireplace this afternoon so they'd be all ready for us. Just have to light the match."

The living room was Juliet's favorite place. Three large windows on each of two sides made it a bright cheery enclosure during the day. When the burgundy curtains were drawn at night, it transformed into a cozy haven. An interior wall featured floor to ceiling shelves filled with pictures and miscellanea collected by the couple over the years. Their family photos spanned eras from newlywed to the last family vacation on Nantucket, when all three kids were able to visit for a few days at the same time. None of the photos on the shelf were taken by professionals. The photographer was Juliet. She had concerned herself primarily with recording the happiness of her family. No one thought to provide a record of hers.

Skillman put his arm over the top of the couch and rested it on her shoulders.

"It's been a good run, Jewels."

"It has been a good run, Skill." She relaxed back onto his chest.

Neither of them dared ask whether their "run" was over. Instead, they sipped from the cordial glasses and surrendered themselves to the glow and warmth of the fire.

It didn't take long for thoughts of Charles to surface. Sitting so close to Skillman, Juliet hesitated to indulge herself, even though she knew he could not possibly read her mind. The memory of torrid nights in the cottage was arousing, so when Skillman leaned over to kiss her, she responded.

The little glass of almond liquor had demolished whatever inhibition she still harbored. Before considering the wisdom of her actions, she found herself naked in the master bedroom, experimenting with Skill as never before. Juliet abandoned herself to what now came naturally; her husband responded the way any man would. When they were spent, Skillman's steady snore filled the air. Gingerly detaching herself from him, she moved to the far side of the bed where she puffed muffled sobs and cried tears of self-loathing, drenching her pillow.

An hour later, still unable to sleep, she heard the girls arrive home. Subdued commotion in the kitchen and bathroom followed, then renewed silence as they retired to their respective bedrooms.

At one-thirty in the morning. Juliet flipped her pillow and lay on her back, struggling to breathe through congestion brought on by the protracted cry. She was calm now, as so often happens when emotions are allowed to run their course.

The moon cast squares of blue light through the window panes and over the bed, just as it had a few short weeks ago when Juliet first went to Charles Westfall. She put her hands on her breasts and moved them down the front of her body, wishing her hands were his.

A car drove onto the icy driveway just outside her window and boisterous farewells followed. She heard the kitchen door open and shut one more time as Jonus made his wobbly way up the stairs to his room. The house quickly settled again.

It was three o'clock when Juliet got up to use the toilet, tiptoeing across the cold wood floor, closing the squeaky door as quietly as possible. The reflection in the mirror revealed her story: hair snarled into mats from the swirl of earlier amorous activity; tired shoulders sagging; lax breasts. She opened the bathroom door and dragged herself back to bed.

Juliet reached over the bedside table and turned the clock to face her. It was almost nine. Skillman was no longer in bed and there were signs he had already begun his usual Saturday routine. Pulling back the covers, she walked wearily into the bathroom and gasped at what the mirror revealed: eyes nearly swollen shut and skin marred by splotches of red.

At the sink, she ran water until it was ice cold, closed the drain, then submerged a washcloth. She wrung the cloth and held it firmly over her eyes until it grew warm. Sitting on the toilet lid, she diligently repeated the process until she felt presentable enough to venture downstairs.

"Morning, party lady!" teased Deirdre, exchanging knowing looks with Jonus as Juliet entered the kitchen.

"Good morning, smarty pants. I'm just not used to staying up so late!" Hoping to redirect the conversation, she asked, "What's the latest with you guys?"

The kids launched into stories about the night before, complete with recent gossip about their old friends.

"When are you going to rehearse, Mom? Didn't you say you wanted to play in front of us one time before the concert tonight?" Jonus asked.

"I do. But first I need fully wake up." She turned away to prepare a bowl of oatmeal, hoping also to hide the anguish and guilt etched on her face.

For the next few hours, everyone moved in separate directions. Juliet spent an hour walking on the treadmill in the basement—normally a great stress reliever. Just as she stepped off it and began stretching, she heard heavy footsteps above on the kitchen floor. Skillman had returned from his errands. Opening the basement door, then closing it behind him, he walked down the old stairs, each tread registering its distinctive groan. Rounding the corner, he stood across from Juliet. Both searched the others face for a clue to determine the next move.

"How are you feeling?" he asked.

"Okay. How about you?"

"I'm actually a little confused." He crossed his arms. "Can we talk tomorrow afternoon after the kids are gone?"

"That sounds like a good idea."

"I guess I'll go upstairs then."

"I'll be up in a while." Juliet resumed stretching.

Skillman did not move. "Juliet?"

"Yes?"

"I hope I didn't hurt you."

"No. You didn't hurt me, Skill."

He turned and left the room. Juliet bit her lip and squeezed her eyes shut.

D eirdre called out from the living room where she, Althea, and Jonus had positioned ten dining room chairs to more closely replicate that evening's concert atmosphere. "We're almost ready for you in here, Mom!"

"Okay! Thank you. I'll be right down," she responded from the top of the stairs. Having practiced an hour earlier in the privacy of her room, she confirmed the benefits of her initial conscientious schedule.

Halfway down the front stairs, her ears perked up. Skillman was pouring himself a glass of water in the kitchen before joining the kids, when he stopped to answer his phone.

Closer now, she could hear Skillman's phone conversation.

"Hi, Gil."

There was a minute of silence as he listened to Gil Shaw on the other end.

"Well, it was interesting, that's for sure," he responded. "There were about thirty of them on the front steps holding signs but I don't think they had much of an impact on the judge."

Juliet froze where she was, listening to Skillman as he responded to Gil's next question.

"No. Actually, he's brilliant, which took me by surprise. I expected some kind of backwoods imbecile. He also offered some pretty clever legal strategy."

Gil asked Skillman another question.

"Unfortunately, no. There's no way around the statutes and Bernstein couldn't risk setting precedent."

Another chuckle, then, "I know all of us were happy when the bailiff finally opened the door. We couldn't breathe."

Another pause. "Okay. See you tonight." Skillman hung up the phone.

"It's time, Mom!" Deirdre called out.

"Just let me go to the bathroom first! I must be having stage fright," Juliet responded, then raced back up the stairs to her room.

Safely inside the locked master bathroom, she clung to the sides of the marble counter with trembling hands. She couldn't believe her ears. There was no denying that Skillman had represented Charles at his recent hearing. The thought of her husband and her lover interacting made her head spin. Each intake of breath seemed a futile labor to survive. Skillman had been generous enough to represent Charles, ignorant of the man's relationship with his own wife. Charles had known about the hearing all along, too.

"Mom!" came the demand from downstairs.

Her heart labored under the impossible strain. It burst with love and longing for Charles; ached with misery at deceiving Skillman; raced with alarm at the threat of discovery.

Juliet searched for the courage to function. She closed her eyes, willing a slow breath and calm nerves. In and out. In and out. This was a start, she told herself. After a few minutes of disciplined resolve, she managed to center herself; compartmentalizing the recently revealed information with a promise to process it after tonight's performance. Right now, everyone was waiting for her downstairs, and all eyes would be on her. She had brought this upon herself. She would deliver.

Juliet walked into the living room and offered a shallow curtsy to her rehearsal audience. They were scattered, each having randomly selected one of the ten chairs. She sat on the special red velvet stool designed to flex with her movement when she played; a Christmas gift from Skillman. The bow was already prepped with rosin. She picked up the cello and positioned it between her legs.

Juliet moved through the piece with precision and emotion, pouring herself into the rendering. She felt the silence of her audience and their appreciation for her artistic offering. At its completion, she lowered her bow and looked up at her family. They stood, cheering. A tsunami of tears threatened to overwhelm her.

The nutty aroma of steaming brown rice and vegetable with tempeh sauté penetrated the confines of the bathroom where Juliet showered. Skillman was already in the kitchen cooking a light dinner for them, despite the fact that there would be ample food at the event. He was concerned that Juliet would be hungry before her performance.

She hoped the children had attributed her moodiness to performance jitters. By now, Juliet was preternaturally calm; resigned to fate; prepared to face the guillotine or firing squad. Cello playing was of no concern. It was the thought of being among all of Winston's most influential people, wondering who knew what about her situation. She swept back the shower curtain and stepped out to dry herself.

At the closet, she selected the aubergine colored wool dress and pulled the protective plastic cover off. Exceptionally flattering, it also allowed freedom of movement essential for playing the cello as well as modestly covering her legs. The neckline, featuring an off shoulder design, enhanced her assets: an elegant collar bone and a beautiful bosom. It was the perfect backdrop to the stunning amber necklace she had crafted and planned to wear.

Juliet opened the mahogany jewelry box and took out the one-of-a-kind piece of jewelry, laying it out flat on the top of the dresser. There were many claims made for the power of amber: mood balancing; relief from depression and anxiety; confidence boosting. She would need all of that help from this gem tonight.

Necklace fastened, she stepped back to assess her appearance. All elements that comprised Juliet Grant coalesced into this one vision before her in the mirror. Touching the cool and smooth amber oval resting on her chest, she recalled Charles handling it exactly that way. Instantaneously, she drew strength from the impression.

It had turned bitter cold again; the melted slush of the day had refrozen into crusty ripples. After supper, Skillman left briefly to start the car so that it would be completely warm for transporting the cello. Althea and Juliet gathered at the front hall closet, locating their coats and boots. Even though their family would arrive early and park close to the Center, there would be plenty of ice to navigate.

While Juliet buttoned her coat, Althea turned to her.

"I finally remembered that thing about amber."

They had been discussing it earlier in the day.

"Oh? What is it, sweetheart?" asked Juliet.

"The Norse say it's tears of the goddess of love."

Juliet smiled at her daughter, then bent down quickly, feigning an adjustment of her boots, to hide her emotion.

There was a feeling of adventure within the crowded car on the short drive to the Royce Art Center. The vehicle was crammed full of five adults bundled in winter outer garments. The unwieldy cello in its case and Juliet's special stool were both stowed in the back. The young adults were busy chattering about memories of the Center—sculpture and painting lessons, and playing outside on the expansive grounds. Skillman looked over at Juliet and smiled.

He had been kind since his return from Omaha but oddly distant as well. Juliet feared he had heard rumors but couldn't find courage to confront her. Maybe it had nothing to do with her. If Skillman was concerned about some work or personal matter, he would shield her by not sharing any details unless absolutely necessary.

When she considered her husband's thoughtful actions this evening, a wave of affection for his steadfastness washed over her. Their enthusiastic coupling the night before had come as a surprise to her, though. Was even Skillman responding to the pheromones she purportedly exuded?

At the top of the hill, the sight of the Royce Center was breathtaking. Lights blazed in every room and on every floor, reminiscent of its former splendor as the home of a wealthy family. There were only a few residents remaining in town old enough to have witnessed this building as a residence when it had dazzled with uniformed servants, important visitors, and showy cars shuttling back and forth between Winston and Boston. Juliet wished she could have been a guest of the original owners in those days of graceful opulence.

The parking lot was a third full when they reached the end of the long driveway. Skillman turned off the car engine.

"There's still time to back out, Jewels."

Juliet cast him an incredulous look.

"I'm not worried about playing the cello, Skill."

Three young adults silently waited for the next exchange between their parents. When none occurred, they opened the car doors and stepped out into the frosty night, walking gingerly over icy spots toward the back entrance. Skillman carried Juliet's cello in its bulky case and Jonus held the flexible stool.

In the warm kitchen, Susan Shaw, Tanzy Lynch, Lydia Randall and the other board members were busy chatting but stopped abruptly once Juliet and her family entered the room.

Susan broke away and rushed over to greet the five of them.

"Oh my goodness! Look at the beautiful Grant family all together here!" Wrapping one arm around Juliet's waist, she continued. "I can't get over how grown up your kids look. I guess that means I shouldn't call them kids anymore, though!"

Susan was in social overdrive, compensating for the other women who remained subdued.

She continued, addressing Juliet's children. "Jonus, the twins are in the billiard room waiting for you. I know they'd love to see you girls, too." Susan maintained her smile a little too long.

The three youngest members of the Grant family left the kitchen. Juliet bent over to change out of her boots and into her high-heeled shoes.

"Hello ladies," Skillman finally directed his attention to the other women.

"Hello Skillman. Hi Juliet," Tanzy replied.

Lydia approached them, carrying two glasses of wine. "You probably need a sip of this right now," she said, handing one glass to Juliet and the other to Skillman. "Aren't you nervous?"

"Thanks, Lydia," Juliet said, taking a sip. "I'm actually less nervous as I thought I'd be."

Skillman set his glass down on the table so he could hang their coats on the wall hooks.

Tanzy consulted her leather folio, reviewing the evening's schedule. The other women gathered around her, awaiting orders.

On the flip side of the kitchen door, the noise volume increased, signaling the arrival of additional guests. A few of the catering staff burst through the swinging door, intent on their brisk commute between kitchen and gallery. It soon became clear that the location of their small group was impeding food delivery, so Tanzy asked everyone to move out of the kitchen and into the main section of the building. Skillman grabbed the cello, and he and Juliet followed everyone out of the room.

Honeyed notes rose from the harpist in the foyer. The walls of the main gallery were covered with the Center's best art. Each surface featured a different era, from early to modern. The colors of the older paintings were subdued but as the time line progressed, the paintings became bold and bright. There was something in the room to please every palate, even the most discriminating. As Juliet scanned the rich offerings, she was delighted to find her favorite painting, previously featured in the window at Cohort's Gallery, now on display with these other masterpieces.

In the corner opposite the kitchen, a handsome young man prepared his music at the grand piano. Juliet smiled when she saw her own Deirdre in animated conversation next to him, marveling that a woman of her young age possessed such confidence. Although it took Juliet a lifetime to arrive at the point she was today, it seems her daughters were right behind her, given the poise and stature they exhibited.

Pushed temporarily behind the piano was a raised platform artfully draped with a few yards of black velvet. Juliet would perform on it, affording every spectator a good view.

"Where do you want me to put this?" Skillman asked, referring to her cello.

Juliet pointed to the platform. "I'll take the cello out of its case now and leave it here. Can you please put the case back in the kitchen? That way, when I'm done, I can store everything there. I'll want to take a little breather before I come back into this room after playing anyway."

Skillman left with the empty case while Juliet set the cello on its side. She placed the score for The Swan on the empty piano bench. Her daughter and the pianist had left to visit the refreshment table. After a surreptitious look around the room, she settled herself on the platform behind the raised lid of the gleaming grand piano. The receiving rooms were filling up fast; there were easily one hundred and fifty people milling around so far. Executive board members worked the room. To the unsuspecting, this gala appeared to be a celebration of art but Juliet knew it was a make-or-break fund raiser. Board members hoped the two hundred invited guests would either renew their support of the Center or become new members. It was imperative that they raise sufficient funds to keep the institution alive.

When the pianist returned, he settled onto his bench, then launched the first few bars of a popular song. Like magic, the room was electrified and the party moved into full swing.

Juliet located Skillman in the middle of the room, surrounded by a group of their daughters' friends. Apparently, he was having difficulty returning to her through the thick crowd. Drink in hand, he appeared to be the center of attention, sending the young women into spasms of laughter. He was telling jokes. Was he flirting? Mesmerized by her investigation, she ignored Tanzy, until the woman called her name a third time.

"Juliet!" Tanzy persisted.

"Oh! Sorry, Tanzy," she finally responded, flushed with embarrassment.

Tanzy sighed. "Did you find everything you need back here?"

"Yes, it looks wonderful. Should I move the platform to the front at nine o'clock or will someone else?"

"When the pianist stops playing at nine, we'll take a five minute break. The janitor will move the platform into place. You can wait wherever you like. When I'm at the microphone making announcements, you should find your way up here and take your place. Hopefully, your cello is already tuned."

She looked expectantly at Juliet, lips pressed tightly.

"No, but I'll take it back out to the kitchen and tune it a few minutes before I play."

"Very good. I guess that's everything then. Good luck with your performance, Juliet." Tanzy turned and left abruptly.

Juliet straightened her back and resolved not to let the sting of that cool dismissal affect her. She would add it to the list of things to contemplate tomorrow. Leaning back onto the edge of the cello platform, she allowed the muffled roar of cocktail party noise to envelope her.

Deirdre was poised elegantly on the bench next to the pianist, anticipating his needs. Close, but not so close that she would impede his movement, she turned each page of the music as needed. The young man had most certainly memorized his repertoire but would not deny himself assistance from such a lovely woman. Deirdre looked over at her mother and smiled brightly.

Juliet was ashamed to admit her bittersweet feelings as she watched her daughters and other young women in the room. Perhaps she had been chasing a phase of life no longer hers to claim. These fertile young females were incomparably alluring with their sparkling curious eyes and glowing skin. She had been there once. Yes, long ago, but she had been there, Juliet reminded herself. She had passed through those same early and clearly defined stages of a woman's life. As she sat alone now in the crowded room, it occurred to her that this new phase she was traveling through had no satisfactory definition or route. Society's expectations stipulated what a woman her age should *not* be and do: wear short skirts, have long hair, use heavy eyeliner, for starters. The restrictive list went on but Juliet was unwilling to step back into life's shadow just yet. She knew the only one who could define and explore her third phase was her; a frightening, yet exhilarating challenge.

While absently caressing the smooth coolness of the amber between her breasts, Juliet noticed the crisply delineated moon visible through one large window pane. At the campsite tonight, Charles would have brought in extra logs for the fireplace but probably would not be sitting inside quite yet. Still outside in his chair under the stars, pulled up close to the blazing pit, he would study the moon, silently identifying and naming craters, and straining his vision to see as much detail as possible in the vast sky. Holding a steaming cup of acorn brew in his hand, he would sip it quietly or keep it warm on a preheated soapstone rock primed earlier. Not just yet, but in an hour or so, he would rake dirty snow over the outside fire, eliminating embers hot enough to catch a stray twig or leaf that might burn unsupervised while he slept. Charles Westfall would rise and walk through the entrance to the cottage, take the heated water from the fireplace, and wash himself, as he and Juliet had washed each other many times. Standing naked, sturdy, and trunk-like, he would feel the might of his body and the cold air swirl around him. She hoped this is when he would think of her; of her soft body, so different from his but willing to meet him on his terms there in the chilly cottage. She wanted to believe that he saw everything in her that she refused to reveal, granting him impossible powers of intuition to transcend all of the reality they had avoided.

In front of her tonight, was everything Charles Westfall did not know about her. He did not know that she was married to Skillman Grant; that she had three grown children named Althea, Jonus, and Deirdre; that she lived in an old Victorian house at Nine Chestnut Street; that Glennie Callandra was her best friend. He was unaware that she would soon perform on her cello in front of this large group. He did not know why Juliet kept information from him. She realized at that moment that she did not know why either.

This infantile charade of hers had endured too long. A daring new conviction erupted inside her. She straightened her shoulders and pulled in her stomach. She would reveal her life in full to Charles the next time they were together. Juliet rose, adjusted her dress and hair, then walked out into the sea of people.

At exactly eight forty-five, she returned to the front of the room, picked up her cello and bow from where they had been stowed on the platform behind the piano and carried them back to the kitchen. The catering staff was busy moving trays of food but Juliet managed to find a comfortable seat out of their way and proceeded to tune her instrument and review the music her mind knew so well. She felt grounded and serene, in spite of the evening's circumstances.

Closing her eyes, she conjured up the serenity she had experienced living in the woods. Tranquility was hers at last. When she opened her eyes, she was ready to perform.

Tanzy stood at the podium microphone, rolling through her announcements. The crowd was generally quiet, with a lingering rogue conversation here and there, not surprising at a party where alcohol had already been served for several hours. Juliet took another deep breath. With cello in her right hand and bow in her left, she pushed the swinging kitchen door open with her hip. Eyes shifted from Tanzy to her as she took the two steps up the repositioned platform at the front of the room. Juliet located all four members of her family where they had squished together on one sofa amongst the arrangement of couches and chairs. Skillman gave her a hearty "thumbs up" gesture.

Tanzy continued to address the crowd, ignoring Juliet's movements behind her. When the announcements were complete, she paused for dramatic effect, then introduced the cellist.

Juliet nodded to the pianist, suspended her bow briefly over the strings, then began to play.

She performed Le Cygne like she had never before—with abandon—letting her body sway on the flexible stool, freeing her head and neck and moving it from side to side. The low and soulful notes were enhanced by the spectacular acoustics of the old room. Juliet was a seated ballet. The dance she offered was one she had choreographed herself, over time, but had never yet dared perform. Immersed in her playing, Juliet's face reflected the mood of the music. She was oblivious to the fact that the crowd had hushed itself into admiring silence.

Finally, as the last sweet vibrato note lingered in the great old room, Juliet let her bow arm fall to her side. She did not raise her head or eyes while the pianist completed the final stanza. There was a moment of silence, then thunderous applause. She stood and made a deep curtsy, then held the cello by the neck and walked toward the kitchen, aware of admiring eyes upon her. A member of the catering staff held the swinging door open for her. Others moved silently, but respectfully out of her way so she could put her cello in its case and sit down again on one of the sturdy wooden chairs.

Skillman and their three children burst through the door, all smiles.

"Bravo! Bravo!" her husband called out as the four of them blanketed her with hugs and kisses.

When the door swung open again, Glennie and Susan took turns heaping accolades on Juliet. After the small group quieted, Juliet took a sip from her glass of water and requested some time alone to compose herself before reappearing at the now boisterous party.

"Are you sure you're okay, Jewels?" Skillman asked with concern. "I don't mind waiting back here with you."

"No, really, I'd rather just hang out here on my own," Juliet said, her eyes bouncing from face to face. "I appreciate you all coming back to see me."

Glennie gave her a subtle look that Juliet knew was her way of asking if she wanted her friend to return solo after everyone else left. Juliet smiled and shook her head just as subtly, declining the offer.

Alone in the relative calm of her corner in the kitchen, she congratulated herself, believing her performance marked a new beginning for her as a woman. In spite of all that had happened over the last few days, she had managed to reach a place inside herself to find some truth.

Absently fingering the stem of the empty water glass, she listened as Tanzy Lynch began yet another announcement, her voice uncharacteristically high-pitched.

"Ladies and Gentlemen! May I have your attention, please?"

She waited for the room to quiet, then continued.

"I am thrilled to have the honor of introducing a surprise guest to you. May I present the last surviving member of the Royce family and generous benefactor of the Royce Art Center, Leon Royce III!"

"Thank you! Thank you so very much!" the unmistakable voice projected over the loudspeaker.

Amid the deafening applause that accompanied the introduction, Juliet stumbled to the door, confused. A gentle push provided a narrow crack through which she could view the other room and confirm with her own eyes the face she knew would match the deep and sonorous voice at the podium.

"I'm honored to be here in the presence of so many art lovers and supporters. This old house holds many wonderful memories for me. I'm pleased to see that it's been lovingly maintained, because even this old house is a work of art."

Juliet stared in disbelief. It was him. It was her Charles Westfall, Winston's "Charlie", and now, the Art Center's Leon Royce III, standing at the microphone. She staggered back into the kitchen and leaned against the wall, bending over at the waist to let blood rush to her head, a taste of bile coating her tongue.

His resonant voice rumbled over the crowd.

"There is one reason why I've returned to Winston to be with you here. Tonight, I want to acknowledge your steadfast support of the arts and your commendable and successful efforts to bring art to your community. I want to ensure that you will be able to continue this good work indefinitely. To that end, I would like to offer you this check."

Tanzy accepted the promissory note, then stared at it, dumbfounded.

"It's for twelve million dollars," she finally whispered into the microphone.

There was a collective gasp from the crowd, followed by wall-shaking applause. Mr. Royce shook hands with Tanzy Lynch, who looked in danger of fainting.

Juliet brought her face to the crack of the door again, catching a glimpse of Charles. There he stood, tall and strong, clean shaven, hair cut and styled, wearing a black suit of the finest fabric draped elegantly over his sculpted frame. He was a new man.

She watched in horror as Skillman, the first to reach Charles, slapped him on the back and said, "Charlie, you devil! You really had me going! I can't believe you're the same person. I would never have known."

Juliet strained for more, but the crowd quickly engulfed both men and she could see them no more.

Releasing the door, she carefully brought it flush with the molding. A member of the catering crew offered her a fresh glass of water and asked whether she wanted to sit down. She shook her head, then rushed over to the coat rack, pulled on her boots and put on her coat, hardly aware of her actions. In an instant of clarity, she asked the same waiter to tell her husband that she was tired and had gone home, and to please assure him she was fine and wanted him to stay at the party.

Out in the clear Arctic-like night, Juliet hurried down the driveway, slipping and falling several times on the crusty surface in her haste to get away. The blazing house looked macabre with the riot of colors and swirling action visible through the large glass windows.

In a matter of seconds, her world had exploded. Who was this man? Why did he live in the woods? It terrified her to consider what he and her husband might be discussing at this very moment.

Downtown Winston was dark and windswept. All of the stores were closed and only a few scattered lights illuminated window displays. When Juliet reached Cohort's, she paused to catch her breath, then stood there for a moment facing the empty display. She let herself cry at the sight of it, then continued down the street, nearly blinded by fresh tears. Without hat or gloves, she was consumed by convulsive shivers; the hardiness cultivated while living outside was short lived, or was a phenomenon activated only by the bonus of spending time with Charles.

Trudging down the alley, she passed all of the familiar landmarks before arriving at her own home where she opened the door and stepped into the warmth of the kitchen, savagely kicking her boots off into a corner and dropping her wool coat onto the floor.

In the study, at the massive walnut secretary, she opened the creaky top drawer. Juliet pulled out a sheet of paper and pen, then scratched across the page in a passionate and furious pace, ignoring any need to edit or reconsider the words that came to mind.

*Dear Charles, or should I say Dear Leon, or who should I address this to?*

*It is hard for me to understand what has happened tonight. To learn you are not who I thought you were is more than shocking. I gave myself to you and opened my soul to you at great risk only to learn you were hiding behind a mask. Why?! What purpose was served by your duplicitous charade? Did you enjoy toying with me? Did I amuse you?*

*Funny thing, I actually tried to protect you. I thought that the people of Winston would slaughter you, but obviously, they love you now. You have bought their affection.*

*I don't know if you are aware who my husband is and I will not reveal his name in the event you have not yet discovered his identity. He is a good man and he does not deserve to cross paths with you. I may have had difficult times with him, but he never tried to deceive me the way you have. I'm leaving this letter for you at the cottage because this is the last time I will visit. You have made a mockery of the love I felt for you, and you have succeeded in tearing my heart from me.*

Juliet did not sign her name. There was a slim chance that Charles would never return to the cottage to find her letter and she didn't want its contents to fall into the wrong hands. Shaking, she folded the paper into thirds, slipped it into an envelope, then licked and sealed it. On the front, she printed CHARLES? in bold strokes.

Under the brilliant full moon, she set out on her urgent trip to the cottage. Fueled by anger and indignation minutes earlier, the moment she saw the outline of the cottage at the campsite, she dropped to her knees.

What had she done, if this was now the outcome? Without hesitation, she had felt her way through her relationship with Charles, relying on blind conviction to assess his feelings toward her. After tonight, there would be no way to discover how he really felt. She could only assume he had seized an easy opportunity to enjoy the conveniently available pleasures of a vulnerable woman. Intellectually, she was convinced of his advantage over her, but emotionally, she found it hard to believe that he never truly loved her. His gaze, his touch, his words—all were still so fresh.

She circled the fire pit, contemplating where best to leave the letter. Inside the cottage, lit only by moonlight, she could barely distinguish her chair where it was relegated to a far corner, away from its usual location in front of the fireplace. She dragged it back to its proper place and propped the letter onto its seat.

Hanging from a hook adjacent to the cold hearth was the shadow of her long fur coat; she reached for it, then pulled her hand back. It would be virtually impossible to neutralize the smoky stench and sooty residue that permeated the pelt and lining now. She would never be able to erase the memory of how she felt wearing it on the first night she came to Charles. At the fireplace, a glint of metal hanging from the iron cooking hook caught her eye. It was the tin cup Charles had filled with tea and offered at their second meeting. Her cup. Juliet snatched it and clutched it to her chest. She would keep this one memento of their time together.

Outside the dark building, Juliet ran as fast as she could down the path, far away from the cottage, as if she could outrun this story she had written herself—a catastrophe of her own creation. Blinded by tears, slipping and sliding, she caught her elegant coat on a branch, then violently ripped it free.

At the intersection of alley and path, Juliet stopped short, considering the possibility that her family could have arrived home before her, wondering how she would explain her tear stained face, ripped coat, ice-covered muddy boots and wet knees. One option was to backtrack to the cottage and spend the night there, alone. Not a difficult task, she thought bitterly. Charles had taught her well how to make herself comfortable in the winter woods.

No, staying at the cottage was not a plausible option. She would have to return home. Her family would be alarmed to not find her there. They knew her as "Jewels" and "Mom," always reliable, always predictable. Despite knowing it would shatter them to find her looking the way she did, transformed from the image they had grown accustomed to, she had to risk being seen.

Juliet hurried further down the alley, relieved to find an empty driveway and dark house at Nine Chestnut Street.

Once inside, she pushed her coat and boots toward the far end of the closet, then dragged herself upstairs, shunning all lights, still anxious about her family's imminent arrival. She wanted to get into bed as quickly as possible and fall asleep, or at least pretend to sleep. Faked or real, sleep was the only guarantee of solitude and safety for her tonight.

Mercifully, Juliet collapsed, exhausted, and remained asleep until the flabby puffing and intermittent outbursts of Skillman's snoring woke her. It was four-thirty in the morning. For a moment, she considered slipping out of the house to see if Charles had returned to the cottage. Despite his snoring, Skillman was a deep sleeper so Juliet probably could have managed this. When she recalled the letter left in her chair at the cottage, she knew she could not face Charles though. She turned onto her side, away from Skillman.

The moon dipped below the horizon and in the overwhelming blackness Juliet felt like debris in space; floating, free falling, coming apart. A swirl of volatile emotions brought her to this precarious position all because she had let her heart lead the way. Now, it would have to be her head she would follow. With a house full of people to greet in the morning, she would require a good explanation for her antisocial actions the night before.

The clock tower bell chimed five times. Aided by the darkness, Juliet closed her eyes and mercifully found refuge in sleep again.

When she woke for the second time, the covers on the other side of the bed had been neatly pulled up over a fluffed pillow and she could hear the steady and hushed sound of shower water cascading in the bathroom. After a few minutes, noise from the bathroom diminished. There was only the hum of the fan and the sound of Skillman occasionally tapping his razor against the sink, dislodging beard hair and shaving cream. With that task complete, Juliet knew he would return to their room. Her breath turned shallow in anticipation; she would soon learn the extent of her husband's knowledge about her affair with Charles.

At last, he emerged, dressed in his bathrobe.

"How are you feeling today?" he asked, a concerned look on his face.

"Much better. Thanks for asking."

"Everyone was worried about you when you left early."

Skillman took a seat at the foot of their bed, the warm scent of his ablutions surrounding him. She wondered if he kept his distance as a hedge against her presumed illness. Had he not he always kissed her good morning?

"I don't think I'm sick. I guess all that adrenalin exhausted me. After I finished playing, I could hardly lift a finger. It seemed like way too much work to go back to the crowd, and

I wanted you and the kids to have a good time. Sorry if I worried you."

Juliet carefully studied his face.

"That's okay, Jewels. The kids had a pretty good time but I let them take off with the car after a while so they could do their own thing. They were so proud of you."

"I'm glad they were there. It meant a lot to me to see you all sitting right in front."

"Hey!" Skillman straightened He had suddenly remembered something important. "Were you still there when Tanzy introduced the Royce guy?"

"No. What happened?" she lied, affecting disinterest.

"Well, I didn't get a chance to tell you earlier, but on Friday I represented that guy "Charlie" who everyone thought was a hermit. You probably saw the emails from church about him—how he was living in a building that hadn't been inspected and everything else. Anyway, it turns out this "Charlie" character is actually Leon Royce, the last of the Royce family!"

"You're kidding," Juliet said. She rose from bed and began to pull and smooth the sheets and blanket to hide her facial expressions while Skillman continued recounting more details.

"No, I'm not. You know how they say truth is stranger than fiction? Well, it turns out he's quite the refined gentleman. Very well educated and well-traveled. I couldn't get the story about why he lived in the woods, though. He apologized about wasting court time and is going to make a donation to offset the costs. He really fooled so many people."

"I bet he did."

"But, here's the biggest thing. The guy gave Tanzy Lynch a check for twelve million dollars. I thought she was going to drop dead from the shock of it. I've never seen her so flustered. You would've loved it!" he chuckled.

"That's amazing. How great for the Center," she said, wondering if she dared yet change the subject. "Did you notice if the kids were up?"

Juliet joined Skillman in the kitchen where they made a festive brunch for their family's final meal together before they would be separated again. Her husband whistled cheerfully as he scrambled eggs, poured orange juice, and toasted thick slices of bread.

Later in the morning, the family packed themselves into the car once again and rode the short distance to the Unitarian Universalist Fellowship of Winston. In the sun-splashed glass foyer, they approached the designated greeters; typically a trustworthy couple assigned to welcome members and new guests. On this day, Susan and Gil Shaw stood ready. As Susan took Juliet's hand, she squeezed it and looked deep into her eyes, trying to communicate in one small gesture, her unconditional support for her friend. Her behavior was the exception. If other friends and family members were aware of something out of the ordinary, they were hiding it well.

The Grant clan fell in line behind Skillman, following him through the sanctuary double doors, then down the aisle to "their" pew. Settling onto the red velvet cushion, Juliet felt many curious eyes noting the reunification of her family. Although she was pleased to show off her children, on this day she wished that their favorite spot was in back or tucked away in the balcony.

A Bach prelude burst out of the massive organ pipes, shaking and thrilling the room. At its completion, the senior minister approached the podium, then took a moment to arrange his sheaf of papers on it. The gold and red threads of his embroidered sleeves sparkled in the sunlight as he raised his arms and greeted the crowd.

"Good morning!" the patrician Reverend Pritchard called out to them in a crisp voice.

"Good morning!" the congregation responded in unison.

"Today, like every day, is a new beginning for us all. When we experience hardship, or even when we experience joy, it is possible to feel as if we are alone. But, this is never the case. We may feel apart from others but we are always together in the human spirit. We must simply open our minds and our hearts to reach out to one another."

He paused and smiled.

"Over the past few weeks, in our own community, we've seen an example of this interconnectedness, reminding us that what we see before us does not always concur with what we cannot see. A story to illustrate this is evolving right in our own town. In the midst of us, a man has lived as a primitive, seeking to connect with the earth, doing harm to no one. His personal journey speaks to many of us.

Because of that commonality and because of our promise to support our own, as well as others' independent search for truth and meaning, we have reached out to this solitary man. We found him to be a physical giant, capable of graceful coexistence with nature, but we assumed he was diminutive in the way he understood modern life. Our modern life. We assumed that about him without really seeing him as he actually is and getting to know him in his own environment. We judged him—not with malice or criticism, but we judged him, nonetheless. It's natural to look for commonalities in others and line them up against our own habits and traits in this way. When the balance of similarities is uneven, and we do not want it to be so, it's easy to minimize these distinctions and dissimilarities that we have noted somewhere in our rational minds. This is when we leap to conclusions and deny what we see; deciding what we want to see, instead. Who among us has not been guilty of judging someone else in this way?"

Reverend Pritchard paused to survey the upturned faces of his congregation, moved a few sheets of paper from the left to the right side of the podium, then resumed his sermon.

"When we are faced with those whose lives are dramatically different from ours, we often apply our own intellectual constructs to their situation. We assume that those who differ from us are in need of help and guidance. We assume they are vulnerable and will gratefully welcome our assistance. We assume that the plans they have to live as they do are not intentional, but are reactive and haphazard. We assume."

The silence of the room was broken only by an occasional cough and subdued scuffle of feet readjusting on the wood floors. Juliet looked at the row of adults to her right who composed her family. With rapt attention, their eyes focused upward toward the podium.

"When reality surprises us, it can turn our world upside down. How do we react when things are not what they seem to be? Do we continue to deny the obvious and cling to the suppositions to which we have grown accustomed?"

The preacher paused again.

"No. This is a time to learn and grow, and acknowledge that a gift has been presented to us in a form we did not anticipate. When one who walks among us reveals himself to be so emphatically different from what we expected, we should not judge that man or woman living his own life. We should turn inward and judge ourselves for assuming that we were worthy or capable of judging another, even when that judgment came from a loving place.

On our individual journeys, we must reach out to one another to share, taking care that we do not impose our own value system, our own reality, as we see it, on anyone else. This is the challenge I offer you today. In your daily lives, to the extent you are capable, consider the path that others are walking. You may not understand why they choose to travel the way they do but that is not your concern. Your challenge is to honor and embrace the reality of others, even when it is wildly different from your own. There will be rich rewards for fortifying yourself with the strength to acknowledge not only what you know, but even more importantly, all you do not, and may never know."

On cue, the organist launched into the first hymn, prompting everyone to reach forward for the hymnals on the back sides of the pews, and quickly locate page number ninety-seven, "Bringing in the Sheaves."

During the coffee hour following the service, clusters of people gathered to discuss the sermon topic. Many viewed "Charlie," known now as Leon Royce, as the carrier of an important message of individuality and freedom of choice. There was conversation about the possibility of inviting him to be a guest lecturer at a future sermon; having him speak to the youth group about developing one's life plan; creating a lecture series on alternative ways of looking at life; or even expanding the venue to include those offerings to the wider Winston community.

Juliet silently took it all in while balancing a dainty porcelain cup and saucer of Earl Grey tea on the flat of her palm.

That afternoon, the five of them crammed into the car one last time and headed to Logan airport. Juliet listened to her family's conversation but kept her eyes focused straight ahead.

"The guy's cool. I didn't see him before he cleaned up but they said he looked pretty convincing. How awesome would it be not to shower for a few months?" Jonus said.

"No one would go near you, Jonus. You'd be disgusting," Deirdre commented, rolling her eyes and shaking her head.

"I think he was on some sort of mission. Maybe he wanted to prove to himself that he could live like he did. Or maybe he was just escaping a mundane life," Althea reflected.

"Or maybe he was just too cheap to pay for a hotel!" joked Jonus.

"The guy is not cheap. He donated twelve million dollars," Althea said flatly.

"Well, even though he's way too old for me, I thought he was kind of handsome. The fact that he's rich doesn't hurt either!" Deirdre giggled.

I thought you were more into that starving artist piano guy," Jonus teased.

Skillman glanced at Juliet who pretended not to notice him, continuing to fix her gaze out the car window. The effort to maintain a pleasant look on her face demanded all her energy.

When they arrived at the airport, the kids insisted they simply be dropped off at the curb, sparing their parents the time and expense of parking on this crowded Sunday afternoon. Heavy security at the terminal departure doors discouraged stagnating traffic, so Skillman and Juliet exchanged hurried hugs and kisses with their children, then returned to their car and drove away.

Now, it was just the two of them. Skillman broke the strained silence with a suggestion that they stop for an early supper at a restaurant just a few miles from home. As they pulled into the "Sea Surfer" parking lot, Juliet was pleased to find it nearly full. Sunday afternoon was a popular time for family dining; the discomfort growing between them would be somewhat ameliorated by the restaurant's jovial atmosphere.

Skillman dug into his pocket, then fed coins into the newspaper vending box located in the restaurant foyer. Settled in the worn leather booth, he removed the sports section of the Sunday Boston Globe and handed the remainder of the heavy stack to Juliet. After the waitress arrived and took their order, Skillman devoted his attention to a story about the Red Sox pitchers' and catchers' spring training in Florida. Juliet absentmindedly perused the "Metro" section, listlessly turning pages, preoccupied with thoughts about her own situation. On the fourth page, her focus sharpened. There was a photo of Charles handing a check to Tanzy with the caption, "Mystery Man Manifests Millions!" She opened both pages wide enough to shield her face, then studied the photograph and read the accompanying article.

*Leon Royce III, heir to the Delaware based Royce family fortune, presents a twelve million dollar check to Tanzy Lynch, Board President of the Royce Art Center in Winston, at a gala fund raiser Saturday. The no-strings-attached donation will allow the Center to use the funds without stipulation. Lynch envisions an expansion of community outreach programs and the establishment of a fellowship for emerging artists.*

Juliet stared at the photo of Charles, searching for answers in the microscopic newsprint dots that made up her lover's face. His familiar smile, the way he cocked his head, little wrinkles at the corners of his bright eyes—it was all there. The tiny paper check he held was dwarfed by his massive hand; the same hand that only days ago, had explored every inch of her body. What should she bid her own hands do now? Crumple the newsprint into an impenetrable little ball or press it flat to her face and kiss the grainy image?

"Excuse me, Ma'am," the waitress said, attempting to place Juliet's meal in front of her. Juliet looked up at her blankly.

"I'm sorry. Thank you." Juliet hastily folded the paper together and put it aside on the seat next to her.

"Looks good," Skillman said as he picked up his fork.

"Yes, it does," she replied. Other thoughts would have to wait until later. Here was a man across from her who required attention and if she didn't respond to him sincerely, she risked losing him as well.

"So," her husband began, conversationally, "what does next week look like for you?"

Juliet considered the question for a moment. She supposed she would resume her previous routine, having expelled Charles from her life with the scathing letter she left.

"I'll probably work on some new jewelry designs. I should be able to conjure up some inspiration, with spring coming."

"You don't sound very excited about that."

"I don't? Well, I probably have to get back into it to generate some emotion. It's hard to get excited about something I haven't even created yet."

Skillman inhaled deeply. "I was thinking of something new for us to do." He scanned her face, then continued. "I can take a few days off now that that merger's locked in. Maybe we should get away; take a trip; go on a cruise or something. It would be a way to reconnect." He smiled at her, overly cheerful, his eyebrows raised expectantly.

Juliet felt a sense of panic at his proposition. This was a man she loved deeply in so many ways but she was not sure she wanted to begin a new chapter with him. It seemed to her that he was proposing exactly that.

"You're hesitating," he said.

"It sounds like a good idea but I just don't know if this is the right time."

"Okay. Why not?" he quizzed her.

Her eyes grew moist. "Do you think we could discuss this later at home?"

"Fine. Let's wait until we get home." There was an uncharacteristic annoyance in Skillman's tone.

They finished their lunch in silence, paid the bill and drove the short distance to Winston.

**M**elancholy reigned in their emptied home. When a ringing telephone echoed through too many vacant rooms, Juliet checked the caller identification, then handed the phone to Skillman. It was his brother in Florida, guaranteeing a call of some duration.

She knew how she would spend that time. At the back of the crowded hall closet she fetched her soiled boots, opened the front door and clapped them against one another, peppering white snow on either side of the brick steps with sand, salt and dirt. Returning to the closet, she strained and struggled to locate the well-hidden coat worn the night before. When one of Skillman's coats inadvertently became entangled with hers, she pulled both to the front. His fell onto the polished wood floor at her feet. Bending over, she took it into her hands and turned it right side out to better reposition it on the hanger. Doing so, she noticed an edge of pink paper protruding from the inner security pocket. Juliet plucked out the envelope and flipped it over in her hand. Skillman's name was written across the front in flowery purple script. The dot over the "i" was in the shape of a small heart.

After confirming that her husband had not moved from the kitchen where he was enjoying the phone conversation with his older brother, she opened the envelope and carefully unfolded the note inside. An empty foil-lined wrapper fluttered onto her foot. Juliet bent down to pick it up, not comprehending its nature. She held the open note in one hand and the crinkly ripped package in the other, then read the brief message.

*Why stop with one? Let's use up an entire box! xo K*

Alternately staring at the note and the condom wrapper, she heard Skillman hang up the phone. Juliet turned and ran quietly up two flights of stairs to the attic.

In the frigid garret, she carefully shut the door behind her, then walked around the disarray of boxes and forgotten items until she reached the window. From her vantage high above the other houses, she looked out over the tree-tops in the direction of the campsite. The wooden window frame creaked under the pressure of her cheek pressed hard against the glass. It was twilight. When her eyes adjusted fully to the dark, she fancied she saw a waft of smoke making its way up and out of the woods. A shiver ran down her spine, but she embraced the discomfort she knew she so richly deserved Juliet stood that way for a long time; not crying; barely breathing.

She could return the note to Skillman's pocket and go on as if nothing had happened. This most expedient option would cause the least commotion and perfect the marital lie they were already living. She considered the identity of the recently revealed "other woman." She could be a young lawyer, or even a paralegal at Skillman's firm. Perhaps their dalliance occurred in Omaha where Skillman spent many hours in intense negotiations, welcoming a diversion from intellectual tedium. It was impossible to assess how long her husband had stored the note in his pocket, but this would explain the uncharacteristic distance she sensed from him. Reinforcing that suspicion was the enthusiastic flirting with their daughters' friends she had witnessed at the Center gala.

Her stomach lurched at the probability that Skillman's passion during their Friday night tryst was fueled by the memory of time spent in bed with another woman. Recreating those pleasures through Juliet, he would have imagined his hands again on young flesh, the fragrance and silkiness of long hair, the fresh sweet taste of a budding woman. Just days ago, she felt she was the sweetness, the light, the full-bodied wine, the complex aroma, the rich and endless delight. Now, in an instant, her perspective had flipped. In her mind, she had become dry and haggard; tired and inflexible; cold and exhausted; old and used up. A crone alone in the world.

Eventually, husband and wife would have to see each other. The house was not large enough to wander apart indefinitely. At around eight-thirty, Juliet walked into the kitchen to make a cup of tea, just as Skillman arrived to pour himself a drink. They silently eyed each other.

"I'm ready to talk now, Skill."

Her husband took a deep breath, then exhaled forcefully. "All right."

It was all so familiar to a point: the sound of chairs pulling out from the much-used kitchen table; their customary places with freshly made drinks rested on top of the weathered oak.

"I don't know where to begin," Juliet said.

Without warning, the man she thought she knew so well broke down in tears. Juliet reached out and touched his arm, still confused about what he knew, but waiting patiently for him to stop so she could learn more. Face contorted with pain, he managed at last to choke out the words he needed to say.

"Oh god, Juliet. I'm so sorry. I had an affair!" He dropped his face into his hands.

For now, she would be silent. If she produced the note and wrapper, he would bear the brunt of guilt. If she returned the items to his pocket, he would never know what she had found. Telling Skillman about Charles would wound him more than he was already wounding himself. But, what was there to say at this moment?

"I don't blame you, Skill. It's not like I've been the most available wife. I guess I knew it would eventually come to this."

"No, Jewels. It's not you. It's my fault. I'm a weak man." Skillman pulled his hands away from a splotchy-red face to reveal pleading eyes. "It was so hard for me to live like we do." His chest heaved. "Do you want me to tell you who it was?"

"No. It won't make any difference. That part doesn't matter."

They looked at each other.

"I really do love you, Juliet."

"I know. I love you too, Skill."

This, Juliet thought, is what a long marriage produces. We have compassion for one another; we care deeply about one another; we would die for one another; but we want sex with others.

Juliet reached over and took her husband's hand in hers. It was much smaller than Charles'. No, Skillman was not Charles; he was Skillman, and at that moment, it seemed more than sufficient. There was precious value to this man, too.

In silence at the table, they sat holding hands, thinking separate thoughts. Having only her own experience to consider, ignorant of intimate details about other long-married couples, she wondered if others arrived at a similar place at some point in their own marriages. She did not want to lose Skillman forever, but felt sure he would not keep her in his life on less than fully committed terms.

As for Skillman, he was inexplicably attracted to Juliet and imagined he always would be, despite the recent reawakening of exciting possibilities with other women. Only now, he did not trust himself to avoid future entanglements, should another opportunity arise. He was ashamed to admit it, but he did not want to deprive himself of those physical experiences any longer. There were so many enthusiastic younger women.

"Maybe we should separate, Skill, at least until we figure out what we want," Juliet suggested, stroking his hand in hers.

"I think you're right." He choked up again. "I can't believe I'm saying this."

"It's okay," she reassured him.

When Skillman looked at her, she imagined he saw her unfaithfulness. She knew he didn't want to accept the truth, so he leaned over and kissed her the way he kissed her when they were young. It was clear he wanted her and as unconventional as it seemed, they linked hands and walked to their bedroom together.

Before she fell asleep, Juliet resolved to tell Skillman everything.

She never had the chance. In the morning, he was gone. It was a spectacularly sunny day. Outside her window, icicles took turns releasing their hold on the edge of the roof, landing on the ground with a crash or muffled thud. Staring at the ceiling, not daring to move, think, or breathe—afraid even to step on the hard floor and confirm she was truly awake—Juliet knew she had to face the result of what she had set into motion. Adrift in a world of feelings, she assigned no significance to the sound of a van pulling into her driveway, idling for a moment, then retreating.

Mid-morning arrived, and with it, Juliet summoned energy to get out of bed. Naked from the night before, hair disheveled, skin wrinkled and puffy from too much time spent horizontally, she was an unappealing sight. Passing her dresser mirror, she caught her reflection. Waves of terror and disgust floated across her face. Studying her image, she saw a rudderless ship destined to crash on a reef; a social pariah who had selfishly soiled her own reputation as well as her family's. Juliet hurled audible epithets at her reflection: revolting, shameful, immoral. Old. She took a deep breath and closed her eyes. The sight was too much to bear.

Donning faded yoga pants and a tee-shirt, she went downstairs to make tea and force a few bites of breakfast; a mechanical meal she hoped would fuel her rational mind.

Pulling the wooden kitchen door open to let sunshine pour through the glass also revealed a large cardboard cylinder resting outside. Not expecting a delivery for herself, she assumed the package was for Skillman, and frowned at the thought of having to notify him about it. She set the tube on the kitchen table, incurious about whatever had been sent.

After a while, Juliet glanced over at the label. It was from Cohort's Gallery, addressed to Juliet Grant. She stood up and set to the task of opening it; first prying off the metal discs at both ends, then slipping her fingers inside to coax out the contents. The backside of a large canvas roll was expelled as the heavy cardboard cylinder fell to the floor. Juliet carefully unfurled the coarse cloth, its perimeters extending over the edges of the rectangular table. Recognizing the painting she had admired for months in the window of Cohort's Gallery, her breath caught in a quick sob as her eyes coasted over the canvas and caressed the colors. Fresh tears fell at Rachel's kindness. She sank onto a chair, let her head fall back, and indulged in despair.

After some time, she dried her eyes and sat back up to look at the painting. It was magnificent, even without the imposing walnut burl frame. Lifting it from the table, she spread it over the floor so the margins would lay flat without compromising the total effect. On her hands and knees, she noticed, contrary to Rachel's initial assessment, a signature on the lower right corner. Pulling reading glasses off the top of her head, she pushed them up over the bridge of her nose. In meticulous but tiny black script was the name Leon Charles Westfall Royce III.

Charles! Juliet sank back onto her heels, astonished. Just as quickly, she rushed to the closet, impatiently pushed her feet into her boots, grabbed her coat, and let the storm door slam behind her.

Juliet flew down the driveway, ramming her arms through her coat sleeves along the way. She was running hard now, anticipating the sweetness of falling into his arms. There was nothing left to contemplate; no more details to consider. She ran with abandon because all that mattered was that Charles had not completely lied to her and was her Charles again. She wanted so much to find a reason to forgive him. When Juliet slipped and fell on the softened snow lining the muddy path, she bounced back, laughing with lightness and possibility. She burst through the clearing, exuberant; eager to greet Charles. Her chest rose and fell. An eager smile stretched across her face.

The effervescence dissolved once she saw the empty campsite. Stones that had bordered the fire pit were strewn around in disarray; a pile of ashes had been spread thin and raked back into the ground. Juliet turned toward the cottage and ventured inside. The walls of the empty room echoed with the shuffle of her dirty boots. Dazed and disbelieving, she wandered its perimeter. It soon became clear that Charles had permanently left this place they once called theirs. Outside again, she stood next to the large heat-reflecting boulder where the fire pit had been, then leaned back against it and sank slowly down onto the wet ground.

Of course he had read the note she left on her chair two nights ago. From it, he could only conclude that she did not want him in her life anymore. She had been angry and confused when she wrote it, reacting without thinking. Juliet tucked her knees to her chest and dropped her head. Was this man really gone from her life, too?

The sunlight at her back softened from a bright white to a golden hue. She sat so still that a few squirrels, accustomed to the respectful way they had been treated by Charles, fearlessly investigated the area around her feet. A robin stood off to the side, clutching a short piece of twine in its yellow bill. The bird flew up to the top of a tree, then returned to the same spot on the ground again and again. Juliet lifted her head. It took a moment to recognize her handcrafted chair nestled in some foliage, well camouflaged near the robin's landing site. Charles must have wanted the furniture to return to its original state. How like him to leave the campsite virtually the way he had found it.

They had walked amongst these trees so often; gathering lichen and twigs, observing the world around them. Was this really their cottage? Cold and empty; no fire in the massive stone fireplace; no shelves stocked with oats and beans and Indian print napkins. She had lived only in the now during her days here. Wasn't that Charles' advice?

Being truly present in *this* moment left her with a heartache so deep, she found it impossible to stand. A puddle of snow, melted by the warmth of her own body, formed around her.

Hours later, she walked away from the clearing, noting that the opening to the old well was covered once again. In a matter of minutes, Juliet would step out of the woods and onto the alley. She stopped to collect herself and decide what to do. Although late in the day, she felt confident Glennie would be home alone. She needed to talk to someone who would understand.

Approaching the vintage Craftsman bungalow, she recalled with renewed horror Peter's recent behavior toward her. Given the weekend's multiple distractions, Friday night's incident had been relegated to the recess of her mind. She would tell Glennie eventually. Juliet knew how much it would hurt her friend to hear the news, especially after her heroic marriage rebuilding effort. That could not be the subject of today's conversation, though.

Closer to Twenty Chestnut Street, she considered her appearance. Her eyes were nearly swollen shut from crying. She had not showered, brushed her teeth or hair, or even bothered to change out of the old tee shirt. Her boots and pants were splattered with wet mud from her run on the path, and from time spent slumped on the melting snow at the campsite.

Wallowing in self-pity, she failed to notice the slow pace of Glennie's footsteps responding to the ringing doorbell. When the door opened and Juliet saw the familiar face of her friend, tears welled in her eyes.

"Wow, you're really taking this living in the woods thing seriously, aren't you?" Glennie said, leaning against the door jam.

Juliet's eyebrows contorted, baffled by her friend's use of sarcasm at a time like this.

"He's gone, Glennie. The whole campsite is empty and I don't know where he is."

She stood on the doorstep like a stray animal, aware of her unattractive appearance, hoping to elicit enough charity to receive sanctuary from a cold and lonely world.

Glennie sighed. "Do you want to come in?"

"If you don't mind. I'm sorry I'm so dirty."

Glennie released her hold on the door, then turned around and walked down the hall, leaving Juliet there to close it herself. She took off her boots and rolled up her wet pant legs, carefully encasing the bulk of the muddy mess the best she could.

In the kitchen, Glennie faced the stove and asked, "Do you want tea?"

"Yes, thank you."

In an effort to avoid sullying the chair, she reverse folded her coat, then sat on the lining.

Glennie carried two steaming mugs over to the table but set Juliet's drink at the center, forcing her to reach for it.

"Okay, what's going on *now*?" she asked Juliet.

Some women are moody and randomly behave coldly toward others but Glennie was not one of them. She was reliably sunny and clear; straightforwardly addressing obstacles or misunderstandings between herself and others. Although troubled by Glennie's affect, Juliet's own urgent compulsion to relieve herself could not accommodate empathy for her friend at this moment. That would have to wait.

"I can't believe all this is happening," she began, her voice cracking. "First of all, did you know Charles is really a Royce?"

"Yes, Juliet," Glennie sighed. "I was at the gala, remember? There isn't a person in Winston who doesn't know that story by now."

"Really?"

"You've been so out of it in your little love nest. You haven't heard all the gossip about him that's been going on for weeks. Gossip about you, too."

Glennie's voice was cold.

"What did they say?"

"Everyone thought 'Charlie' was a crazy harmless guy, but enough people saw you taking the path from Concord Street back to where they knew his cottage was. So, after you started walking around looking like a mess, they started to talk. Lydia Randall thought you smelled like sex. Susan told me that."

"Oh, my god."

"I tried to defend you whenever I could Juliet, but you know I don't like to lie."

Juliet looked at her with grateful sympathy.

"And, I don't like liars," Glennie added.

Juliet winced.

"I'm sorry I put you through this, Glennie."

"I can deal with that."

"I hope you can forgive me. I never should have burdened you."

Juliet scanned her friend's face, hoping for a sign of clemency.

Glennie maintained her stoic expression. It suddenly occurred to Juliet that her friend knew something about Peter's behavior. Juliet would have to face it head on but there was no reason to hurt her with the cold facts unless it was absolutely necessary; better to find out more specifically what she actually knew.

"I know I'm really messed up now, Glennie. And I know I haven't been the kind of friend you deserve. But is there something you want to tell me that you aren't saying?"

Abruptly, Glennie stood and backed away from the table, visibly agitated.

"I can't believe you're asking me this! What do you expect me to do when you go sleeping around and think there won't be fallout for anyone else?" Her voice grew louder. "That's not the part that really hurts, though. I draw the line when you actually try to seduce my husband!" Glennie hurled these last words at Juliet, eyes flashing.

"What? What are you talking about?"

"Peter told me everything about dinner last Friday. How you kept making eyes at him. Kept touching his foot under the table. And then, when you got the chance, you attacked him in the coat room and begged him to meet you later that night. You're just so oversexed now, Juliet. You have no idea how you're coming across to men. But, my husband?"

Glennie's eyes grew moist as she clamped her jaw shut and crossed her arms over her chest.

Juliet was stunned by the accusation.

"I can't believe you think he's telling the truth, Glennie," she said in earnest.

"There was enough of your hair tangled in his shirt buttons for me to figure it out. I saw them when I did the laundry Sunday night. At least he told me the truth when I confronted him."

Juliet shook her head in exasperation. "But, that's not the truth! He's the one who attacked me!"

Juliet thought she saw a glimmer of doubt in Glennie's eyes. She hoped her friend would believe her, but then again, as she said, Juliet had lied before.

"If that is true," began Glennie, "and I don't believe it is, then why didn't you tell me right away? Why did you come here looking for sympathy about your sordid escapades, when you knew my husband was trying to cheat on me?"

"I'm sorry. I—"

Glennie cut her off. "Look, I don't know who I believe. But if it's the way you described it and you weren't even going to tell me... Besides, why would Peter lie to me?"

"I don't know, Glennie. Oh God. I don't know anything. Nothing at all."

Tears rolled down Juliet's face.

"I need to be alone to sort all this out." Glennie stood and began walking toward the front door.

Juliet picked up the inside-out coat she had been sitting on and followed her. In the foyer, she pulled on her boots while Glennie silently watched.

"I'm so sorry about all this," Juliet said, opening the door."

"I bet you are. I am, too." She shut the door just short of Juliet's heels.

Juliet slogged down the street, through the hardening slush; head hanging, shivering in the damp cold, wet coat and soggy boots providing little protection from the elements. She heard her stomach growl. Having eaten nothing since breakfast, she was hungry, lightheaded and unable to think clearly. Ruefully, she acknowledged that even in a crumbling world, bodily functions persist. Was it not a bodily function that got her into this mess in the first place? Tears flowing freely, oblivious to neighbors' eyes, she continued her desolate gait, until she stopped short at the front door of Seventeen Chestnut Street.

The glow of gas streetlights illuminated jagged chunks of ice heaped around Claire Houghton's front porch. When she rang the bell, the old woman arrived swiftly, as if she had been sitting by the door waiting.

"I'm glad you came, Juliet." She grasped the younger woman's hand and quickly pulled her through the doorway.

At this sympathetic greeting, Juliet released a torrent of fresh tears. Claire helped her remove her dirty coat then led her to a kitchen chair, sat her down, and pulled off her boots. She spread a worn white and green crocheted afghan over Juliet's limp body, tucking the edges snugly around her. Slumped in the chair, Juliet watched Claire's head bob while she set the old black kettle on the gas stove burner to make hot tea for her pathetic visitor. Once they were settled with their tea, fruit and bread, Claire addressed Juliet.

"Tell me all about it, Dearie."

A pitiful Juliet abandoned herself to catharsis.

"They're both gone now, Claire. I've betrayed them and turned them both away. I've behaved so horribly that even my best friend rejected me."

"There, there," Claire soothed her, patting her hand. "Why don't you start at the beginning? I have lots of time to listen."

Juliet realized that Claire had only speculated about her behavior, and if she was going receive any guidance from her, she would have to tell her everything.

"Which one do you love the most, Juliet?" Claire asked.

"I don't know," she sniffled. "I have so much history with Skill and we have a family. I never thought he would cheat on me. But I cheated on him, too. I guess I always thought he'd be there for me. But now he's gone. All those years of marriage do matter. I understand how valuable they are now. He was good to me."

"And the other man?"

"Charles. Or Leon. I'm not sure what to call him. That's part of the problem. I feel like I'd have to get to know him all over again. I'm not even sure he's interested in me now that I know who he really is. Maybe I was just a diversion. If I was, he was very, very convincing," she whimpered.

"I see. So, who does that leave you with, Juliet?" she asked.

Juliet looked at the wise face; into the clear, bright blue eyes nestled deep amidst a crisscross of wrinkles.

"I guess, just me," the younger woman responded.

"Yes. Go to sleep tonight, Juliet. In the morning, you'll know what to do. I promise."

Claire rose from her chair.

"I made some soup this afternoon. Would you like to take some home with you for supper?"

"I'd love that. Thank you."

On the back porch steps, Claire administered one last comforting pat to Juliet, then sent her on her way. Walking down the windswept alley, the container of fragrant homemade soup kept her hands warm all the way to her own back door.

At home, the wooden door was ajar, just as she had left it hours earlier when she ran to find Charles. His abstract canvas lay spread on the floor. Juliet carefully rolled it and positioned it back into the giant tube.

Upstairs, she stripped and stepped into the shower, letting the liquid pelt down on her until the hot water supply was nearly exhausted, then wrapped herself in a velour robe. Nestling her feet into slippers, she returned to the kitchen for the vegetable soup and a glass of red wine.

Afterward, realizing she had not yet collected the day's mail, she bundled up again and ventured out into the dark to the end of the driveway. There were quite a few items in the mailbox, including Monday's morning paper. She dropped the bundle onto the kitchen table, picking through the various bills and announcements, until she came across an envelope of finely textured stationary, addressed to her in perfect penmanship. There was no return address. She put her glasses on and opened it.

The beautiful flowing script was written with a blue ink fountain pen. There was a water mark under the letters and at the top of the page, the embossed heading announced the name of the sender.

*Leon Charles Westfall Royce III*
*My Dearest Juliet,*
*I am not who you thought I was but I have not deliberately deceived you. As you know now, I am the heir to the Royce*

fortune. This can be a complicated blessing. When I lead with my money, I am never certain of the intentions of those who are drawn to me. I've found that the only way I can truly know someone is when I do not entirely reveal myself. There were many times when I wanted to tell you more about my lineage but you seemed to find comfort in our mutual anonymity. At our stage in life, we truly are the sum of our pasts. We both did our best to create a "Utopia of the Present," didn't we?

The future is open for me, but because I have no heirs, my general plan is to give away my family fortune to worthy causes before I die. I will travel the world in search of deserving recipients. Until then, I am at the Four Seasons in Boston until Wednesday. After that, I fly to Necker Island in the Caribbean to warm up for a few weeks, then move onto India for the rest of the year.

My jet will be at Signature Flight Support at Prescott Street at Logan Airport at 9am on Wednesday. Will you meet me there? You won't need luggage; just bring your passport. I'll take care of everything else for you. Leave your car keys at the desk and they'll return your car to Winston for you.

Come away with me, Juliet.

Until then, I remain yours in body and soul,

Charles

The letter fell from Juliet's hands and landed at her feet.

Juliet stood at the kitchen counter for quite a while, staring into empty space. Methodically, she refilled her wine glass full of rich Merlot, and carried it into the living room. Anticipating another evening in his own home, Skillman had already left the wood for a fire, so Juliet had only to light a match to set the dark room aglow with a primal atmosphere, reminiscent of the cottage fire she and Charles so often enjoyed together. She took sanctuary on the supple leather couch, sipping her wine, letting the warmth of liquor flow through her, transporting her to a tranquil realm.

Throughout her body, she could feel the pull towards Charles. Her desire for him was palpable. Catching her breath, she thought of their liaisons on his bed of fur; his strong, long legs between hers, his forearms bulging with veins as he held himself above her. She could smell the faint cinnamon scent on his breath, could feel the velvet smooth skin behind his ears and the draw of his piercing eyes.

Juliet knew this was not a time to lose herself in sensation. This was a time for thought. If she was to leave her life in Winston, she would have to know more about Charles. There was ample reserve when she considered his two personae, and concern that another persona was yet unrevealed.

Her hesitation went even deeper. They had no mutual acquaintances. She knew no one he knew. She knew none of the places he had been.

She wondered if it was enough to want to physically cleave to a man as her instinct begged. Was there ever a time in a woman's life where she should abandon herself to the wishes of her heart and body with no regard to risk or consequence? Especially, at her age.

Sparks flew up as a log crackled, broke in half and collapsed inside the flames. Juliet held her glass up to the fire, swirling the wine within it, appreciating the garnet color set off by a backdrop of flames. She felt strangely grounded knowing that Charles loved her; that Skillman was exploring a new life; that her home was her own; that she was a solitary figure. Tomorrow would be the day she would decide which path to take. Tonight, she would not force herself to make a decision, trusting that a new day would offer a solution, as Claire had forecasted.

The fire burned down to tiny embers, leaving Juliet in darkness. She set her glass onto a side table and walked over to the corner where her cello stood in its stand. She had not touched it since the gala, so she tightened and rosined the bow, tuned the strings, and opened herself to a visit from the muse.

Juliet took up the bow and pulled it over the strings, changing notes at random; hypnotizing herself with low vibrations. Over and over she played the strings. Sustained rich notes filled the room. The cello vibrated between her legs where she had pushed aside her robe. There was no one to see her. There was no one to listen. There was no one to hear. Just Juliet. And, for once, that was enough.

She loosened the hair on the bow and returned it to the music stand. It was almost midnight. The entire house was dark. Her eyes had become accustomed to the lack of light, so she easily located a candle, then sparked a flame with a foot long match from the fireplace hearth. Entering the foyer where the front steps led to the bedrooms, she caught a glimpse of herself in the full length mirror that hung on the wall next to the antique chest of drawers. Juliet set the candle on the chest, turned to face the mirror, and dropped her robe to the floor.

For the first time in her life, she saw herself as an autonomous adult. Someone beholden to no one. Someone who could make choices independent of the needs of others. Someone who could choose to act in ways that could fill her up or suck life out of her. The candlelight played softly over the curves of her body.

This naked woman was not in decay, she was in full bloom! It was not a reproductive bloom—as if a woman's life rose and fell around that purpose only—it was the bloom of a hot house flower. Unique, exotic, rare. This bloom was vibrant; fertilized over decades with life's grit, pleasures and pain. This was the perfect age for a woman to grow, to celebrate, to abandon conventionality.

She slowly turned to the side, then faced away; straining her neck over her shoulder to admire the flower again, from another angle in her greenhouse. She was indeed a thing of beauty, inside and out; deserving a chance to flourish under the sun again. There was no reason to stay protected from the elements of life; not a single place where it would be impossible to send out new shoots. She would enjoy the heat of the sun until she was relieved by the coolness of the rain. Even if winter came again, she would find something new to enjoy underground until she found strength to rise up once more.

Juliet stooped to pick up her robe, lifted the candle off the chest, then climbed the stairs to her bedroom, where she slept more soundly than ever before.

There was much to do. Juliet slipped the plastic covering around the long cardboard cylinder, tucked it under her arm and dashed to the car. Rain fell in sheets, melting much of the snow, filling the potholes of winter-battered roads. Her hands gripped the steering wheel confidently.

It was early. None of the downtown shops were open yet, so Juliet drove first to the Dyson Center and changed into her bathing suit. She encouraged herself to revel in the comfort of familiar sensations and smells of the pool where she had spent so much time over the years.

From her locker, Juliet removed the old garbage bag full of clothes reeking of stale campfire smoke, then carried it out to the parking lot and swung it with one mighty arc into the dumpster. She wouldn't need those clothes anymore and there was no time to wash and donate them. It was already mid-morning and she was intent on a very early start tomorrow.

Maneuvering into the tiny parking space in front of Cohort's Gallery was no challenge to Juliet. Dodging raindrops, she ran to the back of the car, removed the large cardboard cylinder and sprinted the few steps to the gallery doorway. She spotted Rachel on the other side of the jewelry case where the soft light behind her head created a glowing halo of curls. Rachel looked up with a smile, anticipating a customer, but when she saw it was Juliet, she dropped what she was doing and moved out from behind the counter, rushing toward her.

"Hello Rachel," Juliet said with a smile.

"Oh, Juliet! How are you? I've been so worried about you."

"I'm absolutely perfect but I wanted to get this painting back to you. There's no way I can afford to pay you for it." She set the cylinder down and began to remove the protective plastic covering.

"Juliet, it's no longer mine. The Royce Center asked me to send it over to you."

"I see. That was very generous of them."

"Yes, it was. With the signature uncovered, it's worth much, much more than I was asking for it here," Rachel responded. "Would you like the frame, too? It really did look spectacular in it."

"No. But thank you, Rachel. I'm actually leaving town tomorrow."

"So, it's true?"

"Is what true?" Juliet asked, not unkindly.

"I'm so sorry, Juliet. I don't want to pry, but you must be aware of all of the rumors about you right now. I hate to listen to them, but some people think you had an affair with Leon Royce when he was living in the woods."

Rachel squeezed her eyes shut at the end of her sentence, reticent to witness Juliet's reaction.

"It's true, Rachel."

Rachel took a deep breath and let out a sigh.

"What about your husband?"

"He's gone. Turns out he had other plans, too," Juliet said, surprising herself with her calm response.

Rachel hesitated again. Her sweet brown eyes had grown shiny with moisture.

"Juliet, I don't want to push, but if you need any help, you know I'm here for you."

"I know. And I thank you more than you can imagine."

Juliet took Rachel in her arms for a long hug.

When she walked out the door, the bell jingled after her.

She walked the few doors from Cohort's to Blersch's Market. There were quite a few shoppers already in the store. Although Juliet recognized none of them, she had the distinct sense they were well aware of who she was and what she had done.

She made her way over the sawdust covered entry to the back of the store where Mr. Blersch routinely instructed stock boys to stack empty boxes prior to bundling them for recycling. Juliet fitted several boxes into one another and carried them out of the store.

The bank, post office, and food pantry were all errands executed quickly, so by late afternoon, she was pulling back into her own short driveway Juliet set about unplugging appliances and tidying clutter. At her basement workshop, she carefully loaded jewelry materials and tools into the padded case designed for transporting supplies and creations to trade shows.

Back upstairs in the study, she booted up the computer, opened the word processing program, and composed one letter to her three children, personalizing each with a different name at the top. She sent the files to the printer.

Having addressed, stamped, and stuffed the envelopes, she set them aside to mail later. She didn't want them to be immediately aware of her plans. Next, she logged onto the Internet and composed an email to Skillman, proofed it several times, then clicked "send."

Juliet sat in silence for a few moments, reflecting on what she had done, then turned off the computer. After she heard the familiar chime, she pulled the cord from the socket, turned off the light and left the room.

Back in the kitchen, she pulled from her earlobes the coveted garnet earrings, and slipped them into an envelope along with a long note written to Glennie earlier that morning. She had faith her friend would soon understand that Juliet had been telling the truth. Her heart ached for Glennie; she had made a valiant effort to save a doomed marriage. Such a fine woman did not deserve to suffer anymore from Peter's callous dalliances. In the end, she believed their friendship would survive. Glennie would need time to heal her wounds, though. While mending, she would find comfort knowing her best friend stood by her side in spirit, if not flesh.

With no food left in the house, she planned to pick up breakfast the next morning, after dropping the packet into Glennie's mailbox. It would be an early start. She wanted to get enough sleep, so she went upstairs, washed her face, brushed her teeth, and slipped between the sheets, content.

A red sun rose behind the budding branches of the trees outside her window. Juliet smiled at the beauty of it. After her shower, she dressed in the comfortable but attractive travel clothes she had selected the night before, then went downstairs to turn off the water main in the basement.

There was nothing left to do. The car had been packed the night before and the house was ready to be closed. Juliet took a last look around the kitchen, picked up her purse and cello, then shut the door, locking the deadbolt from outside.

Next to her car, a cluster of purple and white crocuses pushed their way up through the bare lawn.

The highway was crowded with rush hour traffic. Commuters sipped coffee from travel mugs and chatted on cell phones. When a handsome man in a sleek white BMW swiveled his head to take a second look at her, she tossed her hair and winked playfully.

Charles Westfall waited patiently, confident he would soon spot Juliet pulling into the Signature Flight Support parking lot. In the lobby, he struck up a conversation with a security guard, creating an easy brotherhood as they exchanged comments about the attractive women boarding and exiting the various private jets.

"Are you married?" Charles asked.

"Divorced."

"Me, too. Twice."

"That sounds expensive," commented the guard.

"A bit." Charles shrugged.

"Think you'll ever marry again?"

"Probably not. You?" Charles asked.

"No, never. Can't see myself with the same woman for more than a few years anymore. Too much work. Anyway, why pluck only one flower when you can have the whole garden?"

Charles laughed. "You've got a point!"

It had been difficult for Juliet to choose between her old world with Skillman, and a fresh chapter with Charles, but she was at peace with her decision.

Their plans were not hers.

Juliet Lenora Hammond Grant had her own life to live. At the broad highway intersection, she left the route to Boston and followed the signs to New York City.

She would make her own way.

It was time, at last.